"CAME DOWN WITH NOT A JOINT IN HIS LEGS AND TURNED A SOMERSAULT."

Frontispiece.

Chip of the Flying U

B. M. BOWER

(B. M. SINCLAIR)

Illustrations by

CHARLES M. RUSSELL

Introduction by Mary Clearman Blew

University of Nebraska Press

Lincoln and London

♾ The paper in this book meets the minimum requirements of American National Standard for Information Sciences—Permanence of Paper for Printed Library Materials, ANSI Z39.48-1984.

First Bison Books printing: 1995
Most recent printing indicated by the last digit below:
10 9 8 7 6 5 4 3 2 1

Library of Congress Cataloging-in-Publication Data
Bower, B. M., 1874–1940.
Chip, of the Flying U / by B. M. Bower; illustrations by Charles M. Russell; introduction by Mary Clearman Blew.
p. cm.
Originally published: New York: G. W. Dillingham Co., 1906.
ISBN 0-8032-6121-7 (pbk.: alk. paper)
I. Title.
PS3503.O8193C48 1995
813′.52—dc20
95-4570 CIP

Reprinted from the original 1906 edition by G. W. Dillingham Company, New York.

CONTENTS

LIST OF ILLUSTRATIONS

INTRODUCTION

Mary Clearman Blew

Her parents had left Minnesota and come to Big Sandy, Montana, in 1889 to look for ranchland. They brought the girl, Bertha, with them. She was eighteen. Probably she resented being dragged along. The high northern plains would have seemed the end of the earth to her. Years later, in a novel called *The Lonesome Trail,* she described the landscape as "great, gray plains. . . . scarred and broken with sharp-nosed hills and deep, water-worn coulees gleaming barren and yellow in the sun."[1]

Her family had come to Big Sandy, as it turned out, during a stasis in its history. For centuries the northern plains had been the territory of the Blackfeet Indians, but by 1889 the Blackfeet had been driven west in stages to a sad fragment of their old lands. In another twenty years the Enlarged Homestead Act would bring settlers by the hundreds to northern Montana to try their luck homesteading on 320 dryland acres.

But in 1889 Big Sandy, Montana, was the hub of the last of the great unfenced cattle empires. Across these gray hills—"these thousand hills," as A. B. Guthrie Jr. later called them—the drama of trail drives, of spring and fall roundups, of bucking horses and range wars and cattle rustlers and vigilantes and—most of all—cowboys was playing itself out as though twilight had not fallen on the open cattle range as surely as it had on the Blackfeet.

Its twilight lasted quite a while. In fact, the North Montana Roundup Association would continue to wield political power along the Milk River until well past the turn of the century, and a few open-range cattle operations would hang on along the river breaks through the 1920s. But whether the girl, Bertha Muzzy, was struck at once by cowboy glamor and tales of the glory days is unclear. What mainly was on her mind in 1889 was how to get away from her parents.

The year after she came to northern Montana, Bertha married a neighboring rancher named Clayton Jay Bower. She was nineteen. Bower was much older than she, and he had had a long and perfectly satisfactory marriage, according to old Highline gossip, until young Bertha broke it up. Whatever the truth of it, there she was: a ranch wife. She and Clayton Jay Bower had two sons and a daughter, right off the bat. But still Bertha was dissatisfied.

About the same time that Bertha and Clayton Jay Bower were ranching in the Milk River valley, another young woman was raising her children and coping with the hardships of ranch life south of Miles City, Montana. In *A Bride Goes West,* Nannie Alderson remembered, "I don't think there is anyone so unfitted to raise children as a tired mother, and I was always tired. And then too there were the effects of isolation and of living inside four walls. . . . There were weeks, in our long winters, when I scarcely left the house, except to hang clothes on the line."[2]

If Bertha Muzzy Bower felt isolated and frantic and exhausted during the 1890s, she left no reminiscences. Instead, she began writing, in longhand on a kitchen table, a novel about a ranch she called the Flying U, near a small north Montana town she called Dry Lake.

How did this young woman with three small children, a spotty education, and few resources turn to writing, and why? How did she find the minutes, or hours? Was she creating "psychic space" for herself, as Carolyn Heilbrun has described her own foray into detective fiction?[3] Was she driven, as some late twentieth-century women have said of themselves, to weave a web of words against the threat of annihilation, against the great gray empty outdoors? Or was she dreaming, perhaps, of another kind of freedom? Of her own money, earned by her writing?

Whatever the case, Bertha Muzzy Bower saw her first novel, *Chip of the Flying U,* serialized by Street and Smith in 1904. *Chip of the Flying U* was so successful that G. W. Dillingham brought it out in hardcover, and Bertha's subsequent life reads like the fantasies of women writing in longhand on kitchen tables everywhere. She divorced Clayton Jay Bower, married another man, and went off to California to become a professional writer. Apparently all she took with her was the name Bower, which everyone, including her own children, called her for the rest of her life. As B. M. Bower she had another daughter, divorced and remarried once more, and published sixty-eight novels, over a hundred short stories, and a lot of screenplays. Many of her novels were adapted for the screen. *Chip of the Flying U* was filmed four times.[4]

Chip of the Flying U has been compared, since it first appeared, with Owen Wister's *The Virginian,* which was published two years earlier, in 1902. Maybe B. M. Bower had read *The Virginian* and thought to tap into its success. Both novels are light and often comic in tone; both describe working cattle ranches and the conflicts between eastern expectations and western codes; both center on a romance between an educated, privileged eastern woman and a cowboy. And yet *Chip* and *The Virginian* are enormously different.

The violence of *The Virginian* includes murder, beatings (human and animal), the capture and hanging of cattle rustlers, and the prototype of all western gun duels in the main street of town, complete with the prototype of all schoolmarms: If you do face Trampas and gun him down, she tells the hero, "there can be no to-morrow for you and me."[5] The action of *Chip of the Flying U*, on the other hand, includes nothing worse than a practical joke that gets out of hand, a pack of children who get their stomachs pumped by the heroine (and serves them right, too), and an outlaw horse that throws himself over backward on Chip and damages him badly enough for the heroine to doctor him. The only death is that of a coyote shot by the heroine.

The action of *The Virginian* is viewed through the eyes of a visiting easterner, who looks for and finds the romance of the West. *Chip of the Flying U*, on the other hand, is told from the point of view of an omniscient author who sees the ordinary, day-to-day West. No mistake here: B. M. Bower may have wanted a piece of the success of *The Virginian,* but she also knew her frontier. "There's more of loneliness and monotony in pioneering than there is of battle," she wrote in 1924. "I can personally vouch for the fact that pioneering was—and still is—about ninety per cent monotonous isolation to ten per cent thrill. It is scarcely fair to turn the picture upside down and present the public with ninety per cent thrill and ten per cent normal, everyday living."[6]

And so, where *The Virginian* is "romantic," *Chip of the Flying U* is "prosaic." The cowboys of the Flying U's Happy Family are first introduced when Shorty brings a letter out to the ranch for the Old Man, James G. Whitmore. Bower takes time to draw attention to what, for her characters, is too mundane to take notice of: the effect of a fluttering white envelope on a cow horse.

> James G. stood in the path, waving a square envelope aloft before Shorty, who regarded it with supreme indifference.
>
> Not so Shorty's horse. He rolled his eyes till the whites showed, snorted and backed away from the fluttering white object.

> "Doggone it, where's this been?" reiterated James G., accusingly.
>
> "How the devil do I know?" retorted Shorty, forcing his horse nearer. "In the office, most likely. I got it with the rest to-day."
>
> "It's two weeks old," stormed the Old Man. "I never knew it to fail—if a letter says anybody's coming, or you're to hurry up and go somewhere to meet somebody, that letter's the one that monkeys around and comes when the last dog's hung." (12–13)

The letter, of course, announces the imminent visit of James G.'s sister, Dell Whitmore, who has, of all things in 1904, just graduated from medical school. Chip, the misogynist, is sent to Dry Lake to meet her train, but not before the cowboys speculate on what kind of woman Dell might be—"a skinny old maid with a peaked nose and glasses," they decide (19), and they plot a fake lynching to fulfill what they suppose will be her expectations of the West.

Alas, it is the cowboys' expectations that are heightened, then dashed. Dell, the Little Doctor, turns out to be young, pretty, and as level-headed as one might expect of a medical school graduate. Far from fainting at the sound of gunfire, or even indulging in a lecture on nonviolence, she astonishes Chip on the drive back to the ranch by shooting a coyote and then analyzing its carcass. "Look, here's where I hit him the first time; the bullet took a diagonal course from the shoulder back to the other side. It must have gone within an inch of his heart, and would have finished him in a short time, without that other shot—that penetrated his brain, you see; death was instantaneous" (32–33). And she quickly sizes up the "lynching" that greets her arrival at the ranch and plays along with it. "Hurry up," she commands, 'so I can be in at the death. Remember, I'm a doctor" (37).

B. M. Bower certainly was aware of the conventions of the western romance tradition she was invading. Chip himself mutters about western romances that get the facts wrong and assume that bronc-busters never take off their spurs; and when, laid up with his dislocated ankle and bored, he appropriates Dell's oils and brushes and paints over her sentimental treatment of a Missouri breaks landscape, it is to replace the inauthentic and prettified with "dirty gray snow drifts, where a chinook had cut them, and icy side hills. . . . A poor, half-starved range cow with her calf which the round-up had overlooked in the fall, stood at bay against a steep cut bank. Before them squatted five great, gaunt wolves" (174).

Bower's description of Chip's painting is, in fact, a description of a painting called *The Last Stand,* by a friend of hers, the cowboy artist Charles M. Russell, who illustrated the first hardcover edition of *Chip of the Flying U* for her. Bower's commitment to Russell's brand of western realism, to his exactitude and faithfulness to detail, is plain. But could she have been going further? Could she have been deliberately parodying the romantic western convention, and, in particular, *The Virginian?*

A famous and funny scene in *The Virginian* occurs during a dance at a ranch house, when the cowboys slip into a bedroom and switch the sleeping babies in their blankets—and no one notices the switch until the parents have driven home with the wrong babies. Their mothers (though not their fathers) are furious, and they descend on the cowboys in a predictable uproar. In a long aftermath, the Virginian and the schoolmarm debate western versus eastern standards of behavior: spontaneity versus propriety, openness versus hypocrisy, the natural versus the civilized, the masculine versus the feminine.

A scene in *Chip of the Flying U* also includes a ranch dance, and children and cowboys and an eastern woman, but with the difference that east-west, male-female collaboration, not collision of their values, is its point.

While their parents are dancing in the next room, the neighborhood "holy terrors" have invaded Dell's office, unlocked her drug cabinet, and sampled her "candy." A stomach pump is called for:

> "I'm going to use this." The Little Doctor held up a fearsome thing to view. "Open your mouth, Josephine."
>
> Josephine refused; her refusal was emphatic and unequivocal, punctuated by sundry kicks directed at whoever came within range of her stout little shoes.
>
> "Here's where we shine," broke in a cheery voice which was sweet to the ears, just then. "Chip and I ain't wrassled with bronks all our lives for nothing. This is dead easy—all same branding calves. Ketch hold of her heels, Splinter. . . ."
>
> It did not take long—as Weary had said, it was very much like branding calves. No sooner was one child made to disgorge and laid, limp and subdued upon the bed, than Chip and Weary seized another dexterously by heels and head. (111–13)

Is this parody? It is tempting to imagine that young woman sitting with her pencil and her tablet at her kitchen table, yearning for success in *The Virginian*'s tradition but at the same time longing to puncture its assumptions. Certainly if, as Jane Tompkins believes, *The Virginian* is a reaction against a female-dominated tradition of popular culture,[7] then *Chip of the Flying U* is a reconciliation of male and female, of east and west. It is a comedy that treats the age-old theme of the tension between the sexes and ends just the way it ought.

Dell is attractive because she is competent and self-possessed, and because she has a sense of proportion. She never has to sacrifice her dignity or "stoop" to conquer;

she neither flaunts her medical degree nor devalues it. Of the Montana State Medical Board, she remarks, "They were awfully nice to me—they seemed to think a girl doctor is some kind of joke out here. They didn't make it any easier, though; they acted as if they didn't expect me to pass—but I did!" And as he reads her medical license, her brother, endearingly "growing prouder every line," replies, "You're all right, Dell—I'll be doggoned if you ain't" (89–90).

And Chip—why is Chip attractive? Is it because, to paraphrase Pam Houston, cowboys are every bookish girl's weakness?

The reason, I think, is also the main reason for the deep differences between *The Virginian*, which is a male fantasy of the West, and *Chip of the Flying U*, which is a female fantasy tempered with first-hand experience. (Not that their readers ever seem to divide along gender lines; I loved *The Virginian* as a child, and I know grown men who speak fondly of their early experiences with the Flying U bunch and of their assumption that Bower was a man.) Bertha Muzzy Bower, dreaming at her kitchen table, must have decided that if she was going to fantasize herself up a cowboy, she might as well fantasize one she liked. Certainly *not* the Virginian, who would bore any girl with his rhapsodizing and drive her wild with his moralizing and his insistence on having his own way.

No. Let us have a good-looking young man who may be aloof—we'll cure him of that—but also gifted and decent, and good at what he does. He'll be certain enough of himself to change his mind about eastern women and to be unthreatened by a professional one; he's only a little anxious about social status and uncertain enough to fear the arrival in Dry Lake, Montana, of one Dr. Cecil Granthum of Gilroy, Ohio. He feels called upon to be masterful only where it counts: in the clinch.

As a reviewer from Brooklyn wrote in 1906, "'Chip' is all right. Better than 'The Virginian.'"[8]

By the way, the University of Nebraska Press has followed popular usage in dropping the comma in the title. For most readers and reviewers, Chip was always inextricably of the Flying U, not separated by a typographical dohickey. Bower would probably smile at this sacrifice to permanence.

NOTES

1. B. M. Bower, *The Lonesome Trail* (New York: Dillingham, 1909), 93.

2. Nannie T. Alderson and Helena Huntington Smith, *A Bride Goes West* (1942; reprint, Lincoln: University of Nebraska Press, 1969), 169–70.

3. Carolyn G. Heilbrun, *Writing a Woman's Life* (New York: Ballantine, 1988), 114.

4. Orrin A. Engen, *Writer of the Plains: The Biography of B. M. Bower* (Culver City CA: Pontine Press, 1973), 15. This book includes a bibliography of Bower's work.

5. Owen Wister, *The Virginian* (1902; reprint, New York: Penguin, 1979), 299.

6. B. M. Bower, "Letter," *Adventure Magazine* (10 December 1924), reprinted in *Writer of the Plains*, 48.

7. Jane Tompkins, *West of Everything: The Inner Life of Westerns* (New York: Oxford University Press, 1992), 132.

8. Review in *Brooklyn Eagle* (1906), reprinted in *Writer of the Plains*, 40.

CHIP, OF THE FLYING U.

CHAPTER I.

The Old Man's Sister.

The weekly mail had just arrived at the Flying U ranch. Shorty, who had made the trip to Dry Lake on horseback that afternoon, tossed the bundle to the "Old Man" and was halfway to the stable when he was called back peremptorily.

"Shorty! O-h-h, Shorty! Hi!"

Shorty kicked his steaming horse in the ribs and swung round in the path, bringing up before the porch with a jerk.

"Where's this letter been?" demanded the Old Man, with some excitement. James G. Whitmore, cattleman, would have been greatly surprised had he known that his cowboys were in the habit of calling him the Old Man behind his back. James

G. Whitmore did not consider himself old, though he was constrained to admit, after several hours in the saddle, that rheumatism had searched him out —because of his fourteen years of roughing it, he said. Also, there was a place on the crown of his head where the hair was thin, and growing thinner every day of his life, though he did not realize it. The thin spot showed now as he stood in the path, waving a square envelope aloft before Shorty, who regarded it with supreme indifference.

Not so Shorty's horse. He rolled his eyes till the whites showed, snorted and backed away from the fluttering, white object.

"Doggone it, where's this been?" reiterated James G., accusingly.

"How the devil do I know?" retorted Shorty, forcing his horse nearer. "In the office, most likely. I got it with the rest to-day."

"It's two weeks old," stormed the Old Man. "I never knew it to fail—if a letter says anybody's coming, or you're to hurry up and go somewhere to meet somebody, that letter's the one that monkeys around and comes when the last dog's hung. A letter asking yuh if yuh don't want to get rich in ten days sellin' books, or something, 'll hike along out here in no time. Doggone it!"

"You got a hurry-up order to go somewhere?" queried Shorty, mildly sympathetic.

"Worse than that," groaned James G. "My sister's coming out to spend the summer—t'-morrow. And no cook but Patsy—and she can't eat in the mess house—and the house like a junk shop!"

"It looks like you was up against it, all right," grinned Shorty. Shorty was a sort of foreman, and was allowed much freedom of speech.

"Somebody's got to meet her—you have Chip catch up the creams so he can go. And send some of the boys up here to help me hoe out a little. Dell ain't used to roughing it; she's just out of a medical school—got her diploma, she was telling me in the last letter before this. She'll be finding microbes by the million in this old shack. You tell Patsy I'll be late to supper—and tell him to brace up and cook something ladies like—cake and stuff. Patsy'll know. I'd give a dollar to get that little runt in the office——"

But Shorty, having heard all that it was important to know, was clattering down the long slope again to the stable. It was supper time, and Shorty was hungry. Also, there was news to tell, and he was curious to see how the boys would take it. He was just turning loose the horse when supper was called. He hurried back up the hill to the mess house, performed hasty ablutions in the tin wash basin on the bench beside the door, scrubbed his face dry on the roller towel, and took his place at the long table within.

"Any mail for me?" Jack Bates looked up from emptying the third spoon of sugar into his coffee.

"Naw—she didn't write this time, Jack." Shorty reached a long arm for the "Mulligan stew."

"How's the dance coming on?" asked Cal Emmett.

"I guess it's a go, all right. They've got them coons engaged to play. The hotel's fixing for a big crowd, if the weather holds like this. Chip, Old

Man wants you to catch up the creams, after supper; you've got to meet the train to-morrow."

"Which train?" demanded Chip, looking up. "Is old Dunk coming?"

"The noon train. No, he didn't say nothing about Dunk. He wants a bunch of you fellows to go up and hoe out the White House and slick it up for comp'ny—got to be done t'-night. And Patsy, Old Man says for you t' git a move on and cook something fit to eat; something that ain't plum full uh microbes."

Shorty became suddenly engaged in cooling his coffee, enjoying the varied emotions depicted on the faces of the boys.

"Who's coming?"

"What's up?"

Shorty took two leisurely gulps before he answered:

"Old Man's sister's coming out to stay all summer—and then some, maybe. Be here to-morrow, he said."

"Gee whiz! Is she pretty?" This from Cal Emmett.

"Hope she ain't over fifty." This from Jack Bates.

"Hope she ain't one of them four-eyed schoolma'ams," added Happy Jack—so called to distinguish him from Jack Bates, and also because of his dolorous visage.

"Why can't some one else haul her out?" began Chip. "Cal would like that job—and he's sure welcome to it."

"Cal's too dangerous. He'd have the old girl dead in love before he got her over the first ridge, with them blue eyes and that pretty smile of his'n. It's up to you, Splinter—Old Man said so."

"She'll be dead safe with Chip. *He* won't make love to her," retorted Cal.

"Wonder how old she is," repeated Jack Bates, half emptying the syrup pitcher into his plate. Patsy had hot biscuits for supper, and Jack's especial weakness was hot biscuits and maple syrup.

"As to her age," remarked Shorty, "it's a cinch

she ain't no spring chicken, seeing she's the Old Man's sister."

"Is she a schoolma'am?" Happy Jack's distaste for schoolma'ams dated from his tempestuous introduction to the A B C's, with their daily accompaniment of a long, thin ruler.

"No, she ain't a schoolma'am. She's a darn sight worse. She's a doctor."

"Aw, come off!" Cal Emmett was plainly incredulous."

"That's right. Old Man said she's just finished taking a course uh medicine—what'd yuh call that?"

"Consumption, maybe — or snakes." Weary smiled blandly across the table.

"She got a diploma, though. Now where do you get off at?"

"Yeah—that sure means she's a doctor," groaned Cal.

"By golly, she needn't try t' pour any dope down *me,*" cried a short, fat man who took life seriously —a man they called Slim, in fine irony.

"Gosh, I'd like to give her a real warm reception," said Jack Bates, who had a reputation for mischief. "I know them Eastern folks, down t' the ground. They think cow-punchers wear horns. Yes, they do. They think we're holy terrors that eat with our six-guns beside our plates—and the like of that. They make me plum tired. I'd like to—wish we knew her brand."

"I can tell you that," said Chip, cynically. "There's just two bunches to choose from. There's the Sweet Young Things, that faint away at sight of a six-shooter, and squawk and catch at your arm if they see a garter snake, and blush if you happen to catch their eye suddenly, and cry if you don't take off your hat every time you see them a mile off." Chip held out his cup for Patsy to refill.

"Yeah—I've run up against that brand—and they're sure all right. They suit *me,*" remarked Cal.

"That don't seem to line up with the doctor's diploma," commented Weary.

"Well, she's the other kind then—and if she is,

the Lord have mercy on the Flying U! She'll buy her some spurs and try to rope and cut out and help brand. Maybe she'll wear double-barreled skirts and ride a man's saddle and smoke cigarettes. She'll try to go the men one better in everything, and wind up by making a darn fool of herself. Either kind's bad enough."

"I'll bet she don't run in either bunch," began Weary. "I'll bet she's a skinny old maid with a peaked nose and glasses, that'll round us up every Sunday and read tracts at our heads, and come down on us with both feet about tobacco hearts and whisky livers, and the evils and devils wrapped up in a cigarette paper. I seen a woman doctor, once—she was stopping at the T Down when I was line-riding for them—and say, she was a holy fright! She had us fellows going South before a week. I stampeded clean off the range, soon as my month was up."

"Say," interrupted Cal, "don't yuh remember that picture the Old Man got last fall, of his sister?

She was the image of the Old Man—and mighty near as old."

Chip, thinking of the morrow's drive, groaned in real anguish of spirit.

"You won't dast t' roll a cigarette comin' home, Chip," predicted Happy Jack, mournfully. "Yuh want t' smoke double goin' in."

"I don't *think* I'll smoke double going in," returned Chip, dryly. "If the old girl don't like my style, why the walking isn't all taken up."

"Say, Chip," suggested Jack Bates, "you size her up at the depot, and, if she don't look promising, just slack the lines on Antelope Hill. The creams'll do the rest. If they don't, we'll finish the job here."

Shorty tactfully pushed back his chair and rose. "You fellows don't want to git too gay," he warned. "The Old Man's just beginning to forget about the calf-shed deal." Then he went out and shut the door after him. The boys liked Shorty; he believed in the old adage about wisdom being bliss at certain times, and the boys were all the better for his living up to his belief. He knew the Happy Family would stop inside the limit—at least, they always had, so far.

"What's the game?" demanded Cal, when the door closed behind their indulgent foreman.

"Why, it's this. (Pass the syrup, Happy.) T'morrow's Sunday, so we'll have time t' burn. We'll dig up all the guns we can find, and catch up the orneriest cayuses in our strings, and have a real, old lynching bee—sabe?"

"Who yuh goin' t' hang?" asked Slim, apprehensively. "Yuh needn't think *I'll* stand for it."

"Aw, don't get nervous. There ain't power enough on the ranch t' pull yuh clear of the ground. We ain't going to build no derrick," said Jack, witheringly. "We'll have a dummy rigged up in the bunk house. When Chip and the doctor heave in sight on top of the grade, we'll break loose down here with our bronks and our guns, and smoke up the ranch in style. We'll drag out Mr. Strawman, and lynch him to the big gate before they get along. We'll be 'riddling him with bullets' when they arrive—and by that time she'll be so rattled she won't know whether it's a man or a mule we've got strung up."

"You'll have to cut down your victim before I get there," grinned Chip. "I never could get the creams through the gate, with a man hung to the frame; they'd spill us into the washout by the old shed, sure as fate."

"That'd be all right. The old maid would sure know she was out West—we need something to add to the excitement, anyway."

"If the Old Man's new buggy is piled in a heap, you'll wish you had cut out some of the excitement," retorted Chip.

"All right, Splinter. We won't hang him there at all. That old cottonwood down by the creek would do fine. It'll curdle her blood like Dutch cheese to see us marching him down there—and she can't see the hay sticking out of his sleeves, that far off."

"What if she wants to hold an autopsy?" bantered Chip.

"By golly, we'll stake her to a hay knife and tell her to go after him!" cried Slim, suddenly waking up to the situation.

The noon train slid away from the little, red depot at Dry Lake and curled out of sight around a hill. The only arrival looked expectantly into the cheerless waiting room, gazed after the train, which seemed the last link between her and civilization, and walked to the edge of the platform with a distinct frown upon the bit of forehead visible under her felt hat.

A fat young man threw the mail sack into a weather-beaten buggy and drove leisurely down the track to the post office. The girl watched him out of sight and sighed disconsolately. All about her stretched the rolling grass land, faintly green in the hollows, brownly barren on the hilltops. Save the water tank and depot, not a house was to be seen, and the silence and loneliness oppressed her.

The agent was dragging some boxes off the platform. She turned and walked determinedly up to him, and the agent became embarrassed under her level look.

"Isn't there anyone here to meet me?" she demanded, quite needlessly. "I am Miss Whitmore, and my brother owns a ranch, somewhere near here. I wrote him, two weeks ago, that I was coming, and I certainly expected him to meet me." She tucked a wind-blown lock of brown hair under her hat crown and looked at the agent reproachfully, as if he were to blame, and the agent, feeling suddenly that somehow the fault was his, blushed guiltily and kicked at a box of oranges.

"Whitmore's rig is in town," he said, hastily. "I saw his man at dinner. The train was reported late, but she made up time." Grasping desperately at his dignity, he swallowed an abject apology and retreated into the office.

Miss Whitmore followed him a few steps, thought better of it, and paced the platform self-pityingly for ten minutes, at the end of which the Flying U rig whirled up in a cloud of dust, and the agent hurried out to help with the two trunks, and the mandolin and guitar in their canvas cases.

The creams circled fearsomely up to the platform and stood quivering with eagerness to be off, their great eyes rolling nervously. Miss Whitmore took her place beside Chip with some inward trepidation mingled with her relief. When they were quite ready and the reins loosened suggestively, Pet stood upon her hind feet with delight and Polly lunged forward precipitately.

The girl caught her breath, and Chip eyed her sharply from the corner of his eye. He hoped she was not going to scream—he detested screaming women. She looked young to be a doctor, he decided, after that lightning survey. He hoped to goodness she wasn't of the Sweet Young Thing order; he had no patience with that sort of woman. Truth to tell, he had no patience with *any* sort of woman.

He spoke to the horses authoritatively, and they obeyed and settled to a long, swinging trot that knew no weariness, and the girl's heart returned to its normal action.

Two miles were covered in swift silence, then Miss Whitmore brought herself to think of the present and realized that the young man beside her had not opened his lips except to speak once to his team. She turned her head and regarded him curiously, and Chip, feeling the scrutiny, grew inwardly defiant.

Miss Whitmore decided, after a close inspection, that she rather liked his looks, though he did not strike her as a very amiable young man. Perhaps she was a bit tired of amiable young men. His face was thin, and refined, and strong—the strength of level brows, straight nose and square chin, with a pair of paradoxical lips, which were curved and womanish in their sensitiveness; the refinement was an intangible expression which belonged to no particular feature but pervaded the whole face. As to his eyes, she was left to speculate upon their color, since she had not seen them, but she reflected that many a girl would give a good deal to own his lashes.

Of a sudden he turned his eyes from the trail and met her look squarely. If he meant to confuse her, he failed—for she only smiled and said to herself: "They're hazel."

"Don't you think we ought to introduce ourselves?" she asked, composedly, when she was quite sure the eyes were not brown.

"Maybe." Chip's tone was neutrally polite.

Miss Whitmore had suspected that he was painfully bashful, after the manner of country young men. She now decided that he was not; he was passively antagonistic.

"Of course you know that I'm Della Whitmore," she said.

Chip carefully brushed a fly off Polly's flank with the whip.

"I took it for granted. I was sent to meet a Miss Whitmore at the train, and I took the only lady in sight."

"You took the right one—but I'm not—I haven't the faintest idea who you are."

"My name is Claude Bennett, and I'm happy to make your acquaintance."

"I don't believe it—you don't look happy," said Miss Whitmore, inwardly amused.

"That's the proper thing to say when you've been introduced to a lady," remarked Chip, noncommittally, though his lips twitched at the corners.

Miss Whitmore, finding no ready reply to this truthful statement, remarked, after a pause, that it was windy. Chip agreed that it was, and conversation languished.

Miss Whitmore sighed and took to studying the landscape, which had become a succession of sharp ridges and narrow coulees, water-worn and bleak, with a purplish line of mountains off to the left. After several miles she spoke.

"What is that animal over there? Do dogs wander over this wilderness alone?"

Chip's eyes followed her pointing finger.

"That's a coyote. I wish I could get a shot at

him—they're an awful pest, out here, you know." He looked longingly at the rifle under his feet. "If I thought you could hold the horses a minute——"

"Oh, I can't! I—I'm not accustomed to horses—but I can shoot a little."

Chip gave her a quick, measuring glance. The coyote had halted and was squatting upon his haunches, his sharp nose pointed inquisitively toward them. Chip slowed the creams to a walk, raised the gun and laid it across his knees, threw a shell into position and adjusted the sight.

"Here, you can try, if you like," he said. "Whenever you're ready I'll stop. You had better stand up—I'll watch that you don't fall. Ready? Whoa, Pet!"

Miss Whitmore did not much like the skepticism in his tone, but she stood up, took quick, careful aim and fired.

Pet jumped her full length and reared, but Chip was watching for some such performance and had them well under control, even though he was compelled to catch Miss Whitmore from lurching backward upon her baggage behind the seat—which would have been bad for the guitar and mandolin, if not for the young woman.

The coyote had sprung high in air, whirled dizzily and darted over the hill.

"You hit him," cried Chip, forgetting his prejudice for a moment. He turned the creams from the road, filled with the spirit of the chase. Miss Whitmore will long remember that mad dash over the hilltops and into the hollows, in which she could only cling to the rifle and to the seat as best she might, and hope that the driver knew what he was about—which he certainly did.

"There he goes, sneaking down that coulee! He'll get into one of those washouts and hide, if we don't head him off. I'll drive around so you can get another shot at him," cried Chip. He headed up the hill again until the coyote, crouching low, was fully revealed.

"That's a fine shot. Throw another shell in, quick! You better kneel on the seat, this time—the horses know what's coming. Steady, Polly, my girl!"

Miss Whitmore glanced down the hill, and then, apprehensively, at the creams, who were clanking their bits, wild-eyed and quivering. Only their master's familiar voice and firm grip on the reins held them there at all. Chip saw and interpreted the glance, somewhat contemptuously.

"Oh, of course if you're *afraid*——"

Miss Whitmore set her teeth savagely, knelt and fired, cutting the sentence short in his teeth and forcing his undivided attention to the horses, which showed a strong inclination to bolt.

"I think I got him that time," said she, nonchalantly, setting her hat straight—though Chip, with one of his quick glances, observed that she was rather white around the mouth.

He brought the horses dexterously into the road and quieted them.

"Aren't you going to get my coyote?" she ventured to ask.

"Certainly. The road swings back, down that

same coulee, and we'll pass right by it. Then I'll get out and pick him up, while you hold the horses."

"You'll hold those horses yourself," returned Miss Whitmore, with considerable spirit. "I'd much rather pick up the coyote, thank you."

Chip said nothing to this, whatever he may have thought. He drove up to the coyote with much coaxing of Pet and Polly, who eyed the gray object askance. Miss Whitmore sprang out and seized the animal by its coarse, bushy tail.

"Gracious, he's heavy!" she exclaimed, after one tug.

"He's been fattening up on Flying U calves," remarked Chip, his foot upon the brake.

Miss Whitmore knelt and examined the cattle thief curiously.

"Look," she said, "here's where I hit him the first time; the bullet took a diagonal course from the shoulder back to the other side. It must have gone within an inch of his heart, and would have finished him in a short time, without that other shot—that penetrated his brain, you see; death was instantaneous."

Chip had taken advantage of the halt to roll a cigarette, holding the reins tightly between his knees while he did so. He passed the loose edge of the paper across the tip of his tongue, eying the young woman curiously the while.

"You seem to be pretty well onto your job," he remarked, dryly.

"I ought to be," she said, laughing a little. "I've been learning the trade ever since I was sixteen."

"Yes? You began early."

"My Uncle John is a doctor. I helped him in the office till he got me into the medical school. I was brought up in an atmosphere of antiseptics and learned all the bones in Uncle John's 'Boneparte'—the skeleton, you know—before I knew all my letters." She dragged the coyote close to the wheel.

"Let me get hold of the tail." Chip carefully pinched out the blaze of his match and threw it away before he leaned over to help. With a quick lift he landed the animal, limp and bloody, squarely upon the top of Miss Whitmore's largest trunk. The pointed nose hung down the side, the white fangs exposed in a sinister grin. The girl gazed upon him proudly at first, then in dismay.

"Oh, he's dripping blood all over my mandolin case—and I just know it won't come out!" She tugged frantically at the instrument.

"'Out, damned spot!'" quoted Chip in a sepulchral tone before he turned to assist her.

Miss Whitmore let go the mandolin and stared blankly up at him, and Chip, offended at her frank surprise that he should quote Shakespeare, shut his lips tightly and relapsed into silence.

CHAPTER II.

Over the "Hog's Back."

"That's Flying U ranch," volunteered Chip, as they turned sharply to the right and began to descend a long grade built into the side of a steep, rocky bluff. Below them lay the ranch in a long, narrow coulee. Nearest them sprawled the house, low, white and roomy, with broad porches and wide windows; further down the coulee, at the base of a gentle slope, were the sheds, the high, round corrals and the haystacks. Great, board gates were distributed in seemingly useless profusion, while barbed wire fences stretched away in all directions. A small creek, bordered with cottonwoods and scraggly willows, wound aimlessly away down the coulee.

"J. G. doesn't seem to have much method," remarked Miss Whitmore, after a critical survey. "What are all those log cabins scattered down the hill for? They look as though J. G. had a handful that he didn't want, and just threw them down toward the stable and left them lying where they happened to fall."

"It does, all right," conceded Chip. "They're the bunk house—where us fellows sleep—and the mess house, where we eat, and then come the blacksmith shop and a shack we keep all kinds of truck in, and——"

"What—in—the world——"

A chorus of shouts and shots arose from below. A scurrying group of horsemen burst over the hill behind the house, dashed half down the slope, and surrounded the bunk house with blood-curdling yells. Chip held the creams to a walk and furtively watched his companion. Miss Whitmore's eyes were very wide open; plainly, she was astonished beyond measure at the uproar. Whether she was also frightened, Chip could not determine.

The menacing yells increased in volume till the very hills seemed to cower in fear. Miss Whitmore gasped when a limp form was dragged from the cabin and lifted to the back of a snorting pony.

"They've got a rope around that man's neck," she breathed, in a horrified half whisper. "Are—they—going to *hang* him?"

"It kinda looks that way, from here," said Chip, inwardly ashamed. All at once it struck him as mean and cowardly to frighten a lady who had traveled far among strangers and who had that tired droop to her mouth. It wasn't a fair game; it was cheating. Only for his promise to the boys, he would have told her the truth then and there.

Miss Whitmore was not a stupid young woman; his very indifference told her all that she needed to know. She tore her eyes from the confused jumble of gesticulating men and restive steeds to look sharply at Chip. He met her eyes squarely for an instant, and the horror oozed from her and left only amused chagrin that they should try to trick her so.

"Hurry up," she commanded, "so I can be in at the death. Remember, I'm a doctor. They're tying him to his horse—he looks half dead with fright."

Inwardly she added: "He overacts the part dreadfully."

The little cavalcade in the coulee fired a spectacular volley into the air and swept down the slope like a dry-weather whirlwind across a patch of alkali ground. Through the big gate and up the road past the stables they thundered, the prisoner bound and helpless in their midst.

Then something happened. A wide-open *River Press,* flapping impotently in the embrace of a willow, caught the eye of Banjo, a little blaze-faced bay who bore the captive. He squatted, ducked backward so suddenly that his reins slipped from Slim's fingers and lowered his head between his white front feet. His rider seemed stupid beyond any that Banjo had ever known—and he had known many. Snorting and pitching, he was away before the valiant band realized what was happening in their midst. The prisoner swayed drunkenly in the saddle. At the third jump his hat flew off, disclosing the jagged end of a two-by-four.

The Happy Family groaned as one man and gave chase.

Banjo, with almost human maliciousness, was heading up the road straight toward Chip and the woman doctor—and she must be a poor doctor indeed, and a badly frightened one, withal, if she failed to observe a peculiarity in the horse thief's cranium.

Cal Emmett dug his spurs into his horse and shot by Slim like a locomotive, shouting profanity as he went.

"Head him into the creek," yelled Happy Jack, and leaned low over the neck of his sorrel.

Weary Willie stood up in his stirrups and fanned Glory with his hat. "Yip, yee-e-e! Go to it, Banjo, old boy! Watch his nibs ride, would yuh? He's a broncho buster from away back." Weary Willie was the only man of them all who appeared to find any enjoyment in the situation.

"If Chip only had the sense to slow up and give us a chance—or spill that old maid over the bank!"

groaned Jack Bates, and plied whip and spur to overtake the runaway.

Now the captive was riding dizzily, head downward, frightening Banjo half out of his senses. What he had started as a grim jest, he now continued in deadly earnest; what was this uncanny semblance of a cow-puncher which he could not unseat, yet which clung so precariously to the saddle? He had no thought now of bucking in pure devilment—he was galloping madly, his eyes wild and staring.

Of a sudden, Chip saw danger lurking beneath the fun of it. He leaned forward a little, got a fresh grip on the reins and took the whip.

"Hang tight, now—I'm going to beat that horse to the Hog's Back."

Miss Whitmore, laughing till the tears stood in her eyes, braced herself mechanically. Chip had been laughing also—but that was before Banjo struck into the hill road in his wild flight from the terror that rode in the saddle.

A smart flick of the whip upon their glossy backs,

and the creams sprang forward at a run. The buggy was new and strong, and if they kept the road all would be well—unless they met Banjo upon the narrow ridge between two broad-topped knolls, known as the Hog's Back. Another tap, and the creams ran like deer. One wheel struck a cobble stone, and the buggy lurched horribly.

"Stop! There goes my coyote!" cried Miss Whitmore, as a gray object slid down under the hind wheel.

"Hang on or you'll go next," was all the comfort she got, as Chip braced himself for the struggle before him. The Hog's Back was reached, but Banjo was pounding up the hill beyond, his nostrils red and flaring, his sides reeking with perspiration. Behind him tore the Flying U boys in a vain effort to head him back into the coulee before mischief was done.

Chip drew his breath sharply when the creams swerved out upon the broad hilltop, just as Banjo thundered past with nothing left of his rider but the legs, and with them shorn of their plumpness as the hay dribbled out upon the road.

A fresh danger straightway forced itself upon Chip's consciousness. The creams, maddened by the excitement, were running away. He held them sternly to the road and left the stopping of them to Providence, inwardly thanking the Lord that Miss Whitmore did not seem to be the screaming kind of woman.

The "vigilantes" drew hastily out of the road and scudded out of sight down a gully as the creams lunged down the steep grade and across the shallow creek bed. Fortunately the great gate by the stable swung wide open and they galloped through and up the long slope to the house, coming more under control at every leap, till, by a supreme effort, Chip brought them, panting, to a stand before the porch where the Old Man stood boiling over with anxiety and excitement. James G. Whitmore was not a man who took things calmly; had he been a woman he would have been called fussy.

"What in—what was you making a race track

out of the grade for," he demanded, after he had bestowed a hasty kiss beside the nose of his sister.

Chip dropped a heavy trunk upon the porch and reached for the guitar before he answered.

"I was just trying those new springs on the buggy."

"It was very exciting," commented Miss Whitmore, airily. "I shot a coyote, J. G., but we lost it coming down the hill. Your men were playing a funny game—hare and hounds, it looked like. Or were they breaking a new horse?"

The Old Man looked at Chip, intelligence dawning in his face. There was something back of it all, he knew. He had been asleep when the uproar began, and had reached the door only in time to see the creams come down the grade like a daylight shooting star.

"I guess they was breaking a bronk," he said, carelessly; "you've got enough baggage for a trip round the world, Dell. I hope it ain't all dope for us poor devils. Tell Shorty I want t' see him, Chip."

Chip took the reins from the Old Man's hands, sprang in and drove back down the hill to the stables.

The "reception committee," as Chip sarcastically christened them, rounded up the runaway and sneaked back to the ranch by the coulee trail. With much unseemly language, they stripped the saddle and a flapping pair of overalls off poor, disgraced Banjo, and kicked him out of the corral.

"That's the way Jack's schemes always pan out," grumbled Slim. "By golly, yuh don't get me into another jackpot like that!"

"You might explain why you let that" (several kinds of) "cayuse get away from you!" retorted Jack, fretfully. "If you'd been onto your job, things would have been smooth as silk."

"Wonder what the old maid thought," broke in Weary, bent on preserving peace in the Happy Family.

"I'll bet she never saw us at all!" laughed Cal. "Old Splinter gave her all she wanted to do, hanging to the rig. The way he came down that grade wasn't slow. He just missed running into Banjo on the Hog's Back by the skin of the teeth. If he had, it'd be good-by, doctor—and Chip, too. Gee, that was a close shave!"

"Well," said Happy Jack, mournfully, "if we don't all get the bounce for this, I miss my guess. It's a little the worst we've done yet."

"Except that time we tin-canned that stray steer, last winter," amended Weary, chuckling over the remembrance as he fastened the big gate behind them.

"Yes, that was another of Jack's fool schemes," put in Slim. "Go and tin-can a four-year-old steer and let him take after the Old Man and put him on the calf shed, first pass he made. Old Man was sure hot about that—by golly, it didn't help his rheumatism none."

"He'll sure go straight in the air over this," reiterated Happy Jack, with mournful conviction.

"There's old Splinter at the bunk house—drawing our pictures, I'll bet a dollar. Hey, Chip! How you vas, already yet?" sung out Weary, whose sunny temper no calamity could sour.

Chip glanced at them and went on cutting the leaves of a late magazine which he had purloined from the Dry Lake barber. Cal Emmett strode up and grabbed the limp, gray hat from his head and began using it for a football.

"Here! Give that back!" commanded Chip, laughing. "*Don't* make a dish rag of my new John B. Stetson, Cal. It won't be fit for the dance."

"Gee! It don't lack much of being a dish rag, now, if I'm any judge. Now! Great Scott!" He held it at arm's length and regarded it derisively.

"Well, it was new two years ago," explained Chip, making an ineffectual grab at it.

Cal threw it to him and came and sat down upon his heels to peer over Chip's arm at the magazine.

"How's the old maid doctor?" asked Jack Bates, leaning against the door while he rolled a cigarette.

"Scared plum to death. I left the remains in the Old Man's arms."

"Was she scared, honest?" Cal left off studying the "Types of Fair Women."

"What did she say when we broke loose?" Jack drew a match sharply along a log.

"Nothing. Well, yes, she said 'Are they going to *h-a-n-g* that man?'" Chip's voice quavered the words in a shrill falsetto.

"The deuce she did!" Jack indulged in a gratified laugh.

"What did she say when you put the creams under the whip, up there? I don't suppose the old girl is wise to the fact that you saved her neck right then—but you sure did. You done yourself proud, Splinter." Cal patted Chip's knee approvingly.

Chip blushed under the praise and hastily answered the question.

"She hollered out: '*Stop!* There goes my *coyote!*'"

"Her *coyote?*"

"*Her* coyote?"

"What the devil was she doing with a *coyote?*"

The Happy Family stood transfixed, and Chip's eyes were seen to laugh.

"Her COYOTE. Did any of you fellows happen to see a dead coyote up on the grade? Because if you did, it's the doctor's."

Weary Willie walked deliberately over and seized Chip by the shoulders, bringing him to his feet with one powerful yank.

"Don't you try throwing any loads into *this* crowd, young man. Answer me truly—s'help yuh. How did that old maid come by a coyote—a dead one?"

Chip squirmed loose and reached for his cigarette book. "She shot it," he said, calmly, but with twitching lips.

"Shot it!" Five voices made up the incredulous echo.

"What with?" demanded Weary when he got his breath.

"With my rifle. I brought it out from town today. Bert Rogers had left it at the barber shop for me."

"Gee whiz! And them creams hating a gun like poison! She didn't shoot from the rig, did she?"

"Yes," said Chip, "she did. The first time she didn't know any better—and the second time she was hot at me for hinting she was scared. She's a spunky little devil, all right. She's busy hating me right now for running the grade—thinks I did it to scare her, I guess. That's all some fool women know."

"She's a howling sport, then!" groaned Cal, who much preferred the Sweet Young Things.

"No—I sized her up as a maverick."

"What does she look like?"

"How old is she?"

"I never asked her age," replied Chip, his face lighting briefly in a smile. "As to her looks, she isn't cross-eyed, and she isn't four-eyed. That's as much as I noticed." After this bald lie he became busy with his cigarette. "Give me that magazine, Cal. I didn't finish cutting the leaves."

CHAPTER III.

Silver.

Miss Della Whitmore gazed meditatively down the hill at the bunk house. The boys were all at work, she knew. She had heard J. G. tell two of them to "ride the sheep coulee fence," and had been consumed with amazed curiosity at the order. Wherefore should two sturdy young men be commanded to ride a fence, when there were horses that assuredly needed exercise—judging by their antics—and needed it badly? She resolved to ask J. G. at the first opportunity.

The others were down at the corrals, branding a few calves which belonged on the home ranch. She had announced her intention of going to look on, and her brother, knowing how the boys would regard her presence, had told her plainly that they did not want her. He said it was no place for girls, anyway. Then he had put on a very dirty pair of overalls and hurried down to help for he was not above lending a hand when there was extra work to be done.

Miss Della Whitmore tidied the kitchen and dusted the sitting room, and then, having a pair of mischievously idle hands and a very feminine curiosity, conceived an irrepressible desire to inspect the bunk house.

J. G. would tell her that, also, was no place for girls, she supposed, but J. G. was not present, so his opinion did not concern her. She had been at the Flying U ranch a whole week, and was beginning to feel that its resources for entertainment—aside from the masculine contingent, which held some promising material—were about exhausted. She had climbed the bluffs which hemmed the coulee on either side, had selected her own private saddle horse, a little sorrel named Concho, and had made friends with Patsy, the cook. She had dazzled Cal Emmett with her wiles and had found occasion to show Chip how little she thought of him; a highly unsatisfactory achievement, since Chip calmly overlooked her whenever common politeness permitted him.

There yet remained the unexplored mystery of that little cabin down the slope, from which sounded so much boylike laughter of an evening. She watched and waited till she was positive the coast was clear, then clapped an old hat of J. G.'s upon her head and ran lightly down the hill.

With her hand upon the knob, she ran her eye critically along the outer wall and decided that it had, at some remote date, been treated to a coat of whitewash; gave the knob a sudden twist, with a backward glance like a child stealing cookies, stepped in and came near falling headlong. She had not expected that remoteness of floor common to cabins built on a side hill.

"Well!" She pulled herself together and looked curiously about her. What struck her at first was the total absence of bunks. There were a couple of plain, iron bedsteads and two wooden ones made of rough planks. There was a funny-looking table made of an inverted coffee box with legs of two-by-four, and littered with a charactertistic collection of bachelor trinkets. There was a glass lamp with a badly smoked chimney, a pack of cards, a sack of smoking tobacco and a box of matches. There was a tin box with spools of very coarse thread, some equally coarse needles and a pair of scissors. There was also—and Miss Whitmore gasped when she saw it—a pile of much-read magazines with the latest number of her favorite upon the top. She went closer and examined them, and glanced around the room with doubting eyes. There were spurs, quirts, chaps and queer-looking bits upon the walls; there were cigarette stubs and burned matches innumerable upon the rough, board floor, and here in her hand—she turned the pages of her favorite abstractedly and a paper fluttered out and fell, face upward, on the floor. She stooped and recovered it, glanced and gasped.

"Well!"

It was only a pencil sketch done on cheap, unruled tablet paper, but her mind dissolved into a chaos of interrogation marks and exclamation points—with the latter predominating more and more the longer she looked.

It showed blunt-topped hills and a shallow coulee which she remembered perfectly. In the foreground a young woman in a smart tailored costume, the accuracy of which was something amazing, stood proudly surveying a dead coyote at her feet. In a corner of the picture stood a weather-beaten stump with a long, thin splinter beside it on the ground. Underneath was written in characters beautifully symmetrical: "The old maid's credential card."

There was no gainsaying the likeness; even the rakish tilt of the jaunty felt hat, caused by the wind and that wild dash across country, was painstakingly reproduced. And the fanciful tucks on the sleeve of the gown—"and I didn't suppose he had deigned so much as a glance!" was her first coherent thought.

Miss Whitmore's soul burned with resentment. No woman, even at twenty-three, loves to be called "the old maid"—especially by a keen-witted young man with square chin and lips with a pronounced curve to them. And whoever supposed the fellow could draw like that—and notice every tiny little detail without really looking once? Of course, she knew her hat was crooked, with the wind blowing one's head off, almost, but he had no business: "The old maid's credential card!"—"Old maid," indeed!

"The audacity of him!"

"Beg pardon?"

Miss Whitmore wheeled quickly, her heart in the upper part of her throat, judging by the feel of it. Chip himself stood just inside the door, eying her coldly.

"I was not speaking," said Miss Whitmore, haughtily, in futile denial.

To this surprising statement Chip had nothing to say. He went to one of the iron beds, stooped and drew out a bundle which, had Miss Whitmore asked him what it was, he would probably have called his "war sack." She did not ask; she stood and watched him, though her conscience assured her it was a dreadfully rude thing to do, and that her place was up at the house. Miss Whitmore was frequently at odds with her conscience; at this time she stood her ground, backed by her pride, which was her chiefest ally in such emergencies.

When he drew a huge, murderous-looking revolver from its scabbard and proceeded calmly to insert cartridge after cartridge, Miss Whitmore was constrained to speech.

"Are you—going to—*shoot* something?"

The question struck them both as particularly inane, in view of his actions.

"I am," replied he, without looking up. He whirled the cylinder into place, pushed the bundle back under the bed and rose, polishing the barrel of the gun with a silk handkerchief.

Miss Whitmore hoped he wasn't going to murder anyone; he looked keyed up to almost any desperate deed.

"Who—what are you going to shoot?" Really, the question asked itself.

Chip raised his eyes for a fleeting glance which took in the pencil sketch in her hand. Miss Whitmore observed that his eyes were much darker than hazel; they were almost black. And there was, strangely enough, not a particle of curve to his lips; they were thin, and straight, and stern.

"Silver. He broke his leg."

"Oh!" There was real horror in her tone. Miss Whitmore knew all about Silver from garrulous Patsy. Chip had rescued a pretty, brown colt from starving on the range, had bought him of the owner, petted and cared for him until he was now one of the best saddle horses on the ranch. He was a dark chestnut, with beautiful white, crinkly mane and tail and white feet. Miss Whitmore had seen Chip riding him down the coulee trail only yesterday, and now—— Her heart ached with the pity of it.

"How did it happen?"

"I don't know. He was in the little pasture. Got kicked, maybe." Chip jerked open the door with a force greatly in excess of the need of it.

Miss Whitmore started impulsively toward him. Her eyes were not quite clear.

"Don't—not yet! Let me go. If it's a straight break I can set the bone and save him."

Chip, savage in his misery, regarded her over one square shoulder.

"Are you a veterinary surgeon, may I ask?"

Miss Whitmore felt her cheeks grow hot, but she stood her ground.

"I am not. But a broken bone is a broken bone, whether it belongs to a man—or some *other* beast!"

"Y-e-s?"

Chip's way of saying yes was one of his chief weapons of annihilation. He had a peculiar, taunting inflection which he could give to it, upon occasion, which caused prickles of flesh upon the victim. To say that Miss Whitmore was not utterly quenched argues well for her courage. She only gasped, as though treated to an unexpected dash of cold water, and went on.

"I'm sure I might save him if you'd let me try. Or are you really eager to shoot him?"

Chip's muscles shrank. Eager to shoot him—

Silver, the only thing that loved and understood him?

"You may come and look at him, if you like," he said, after a breath or two.

Miss Whitmore overlooked the tolerance of the tone and stepped to his side, mechanically clutching the sketch in her fingers. It was Chip, looking down at her from his extra foot of height, who called her attention to it.

"Are you thinking of using that for a plaster?"

Miss Whitmore started and blushed, then, with an uptilt of chin:

"If I need a strong irritant, yes!" She calmly rolled the paper into a tiny tube and thrust it into the front of her pink shirt-waist for want of a pocket —and Chip, watching her surreptitiously, felt a queer grip in his chest, which he thought it best to set down as anger.

Silently they hurried down where Silver lay, his beautiful, gleaming mane brushing the tender green of the young grass blades. He lifted his head when he heard Chip's step, and neighed wistfully. Chip bent over him, black agony in his eyes. Miss Whitmore, looking on, realized for the first time that the suffering of the horse was a mere trifle compared to that of his master. Her eyes wandered to the loaded revolver which bulged his pocket behind, and she shuddered—but not for Silver. She went closer and laid her hand upon the shimmery mane. The horse snorted nervously and struggled to rise.

"He's not used to a woman," said Chip, with a certain accent of pride. "I guess this is the closest he's ever been to one. You see, he's never had any one handle him but me."

"Then he certainly is no lady's horse," said Miss Whitmore, good-naturedly. Somehow, in the last moment, her attitude toward Chip had changed considerably. "Try and make him let me feel the break."

With much coaxing and soothing words it was accomplished, and it did not take long, for it was a front leg, broken straight across, just above the fetlock. Miss Whitmore stood up and smiled into the young man's eyes, conscious of a desire to bring the curve back into his lips.

"It's very simple," she declared, cheerfully. "I know I can cure him. We had a colt at home with his leg broken the same way, and he was entirely cured—and doesn't even limp. Of course," she added, honestly, "Uncle John doctored him—but I helped."

Chip drew the back of his gloved hand quickly across his eyes and swallowed.

"Miss Whitmore—if you could save old Silver——"

Miss Whitmore, the self-contained young medical graduate, blinked rapidly and found urgent need of tucking in wind-blown, brown locks, with her back to the tall cow-puncher who had unwittingly dropped his mask for an instant. She took off J. G.'s old hat, turned it clean around twice and put it back exactly as it was before; unless the tilt over her left ear was a trifle more pronounced. Show me the woman who can set a hat straight upon her head without aid of a mirror!

"We must get him up from there and into a box stall. There is one, isn't there?"

"Y-e-s——" Chip hesitated. "I wouldn't ask the Old—your brother, for the use of it, though; not even for Silver."

"I will," returned she, promptly. "I never feel any compunction about asking for what I want—if I can't get it any other way. I can't understand why you wanted to shoot—you must have known this bone could be set."

"I didn't *want* to——" Chip bent over and drove a fly from Silver's shoulder. "When a horse belonging to the outfit gets crippled like that, he makes coyote bait. A forty-dollar cow-puncher can't expect any better for his own horse."

"He'll *get* better, whatever he may expect. I'm just spoiling for something to practice on, anyway—and he's such a beauty. If you can get him up, lead him to the stable while I go and tell J. G. and get some one to help." She started away.

"Whom shall I get?" she called back.

"Weary, if you can—and Slim's a good hand with horses, too."

"Slim—is that the tall, lanky man?"

"No—he's the short, fat one. That bean-pole is Shorty."

Miss Whitmore fixed these facts firmly in her memory and ran swiftly to where rose all the dust and noise from the further corral. She climbed up until she could look conveniently over the top rail. The fence seemed to her dreadfully high—a clean waste of straight, sturdy poles.

"J. G-e-e-e!"

"Baw-h-h-h!" came answer from a wholly unexpected source as a big, red cow charged and struck the fence under her feet a blow which nearly dislodged her from her perch. The cow recoiled a few steps and lowered her head truculently.

"Scat! Shoo, there! Go on away, you horrid old thing you! Oh, J. G-e-e-e!"

Weary, who was roping, had just dragged a calf up to the fire and was making a loop to catch another when the cow made a second charge at the fence. He dashed in ahead of her, his horse narrowly escaping an ugly gash from her long, wicked horns. As he dodged he threw his rope with the peculiar, back-hand twist of the practiced roper, catching her by the head and one front foot. Straight across the corral he shot to the end of a forty-foot rope tied fast to the saddle horn. The red cow flopped with a thump which knocked all desire for trouble out of her for the time. Shorty slipped the rope off and climbed the fence, but the cow only shook her aching sides and limped sullenly away to the far side of the corral. J. G. and the boys had shinned up the fence like scared cats up a tree when the trouble began, and perched in a row upon the top. The Old Man looked across and espied his sister, wide-eyed and undignified, watching the outcome.

"Dell! What in thunder the *you* doing on that fence?" he shouted across the corral.

"What in thunder are you doing on the fence, J G.?" she flung back at him.

The Old Man climbed shamefacedly down, followed by the others. "Is that what you call 'getting put in the clear'?" asked she, genially. "I see now—it means clear on the top rail."

"You go back to the house and stay there!" commanded J. G., wrathfully. The boys were showing unmistakable symptoms of mirth, and the laugh was plainly against the Old Man.

"Oh, no," came her voice, honey-sweet and calm. "Shoo that cow this way again, will you, Mr. Weary? I like to watch J. G. shin up the fence. It's good for him; it makes one supple, and J. G.'s actually getting fat."

"Hurry along with that calf!" shouted the Old Man, recovering the branding iron and turning his back on his tormentor.

The boys, beyond grinning furtively at one another, behaved with quite praiseworthy gravity. Miss Whitmore watched while Weary dragged a spotted calf up to the fire and the boys threw it to the ground and held it until the Old Man had stamped it artistically with a smoking U.

"Oh, J. G.!"

"Ain't you gone yet? What d'yuh want?"

"Silver broke his leg."

"Huh. I knew that long ago. Chip's gone to shoot him. You go on to the house, doggone it! You'll have every cow in the corral on the fight. That red waist of yours——"

"It isn't red, it's pink—a beautiful rose pink. If your cows don't like it, they'll have to be educated up to it. Chip isn't either going to shoot that horse, J. G. I'm going to set his leg and cure him—and I'm going to keep him in one of your box stalls. There, now!"

Cal Emmett took a sudden fit of coughing and leaned his forehead weakly against a rail, and Weary got into some unnecessary argument with his horse and bolted across to the gate, where his shoulders were seen to shake—possibly with a nervous chill; the bravest riders are sometimes so affected. Nobody laughed, however. Indeed, Slim seemed unusually serious, even for him, while Happy Jack looked positively in pain.

"I want that short, fat man to help" (Slim

squirmed at this blunt identification of himself) "and Mr. Weary, also." Miss Whitmore might have spoken with a greater effect of dignity had she not been clinging to the top of the fence with two dainty slipper toes thrust between the rails not so very far below. Under the circumstances, she looked like a pretty, spoiled little schoolgirl.

"Oh. You've turned horse doctor, have yuh?" J. G. leaned suddenly upon his branding iron and laughed. "Doggone it, that ain't a bad idea. I've got two box stalls, and there's an old gray horse in the pasture—the same old gray horse that come out uh the wilderness—with a bad case uh string-halt. I'll have some uh the boys ketch him up and you can start a horsepital!"

"Is that supposed to be a joke, J. G.? I never can tell *your* jokes by ear. If it is, I'll laugh. I'm going to use whatever I need and you can do without Mr.—er—those two men."

"Oh, go ahead. The horse don't belong to *me*, so I'm willing you should practice on him a while. Say! Dell! Give him that truck you've been pouring down me for the last week. Maybe he'll relish the taste of the doggone stuff—I don't."

"I suppose you've labeled *that* a 'Joke—please laugh here,'" sighed Miss Whitmore, plaintively, climbing gingerly down.

CHAPTER IV.

An Ideal Picture.

"I guess I'll go down to Denson's to-day," said J. G. at the breakfast table one morning. "Maybe we can get that grass widow to come and keep house for us."

"I don't want any old grass widow to keep house," protested Della. "I'm getting along well enough, so long as Patsy bakes the bread, and meat, and cake, and stuff. It's just fun to keep house. The only trouble is, there isn't half enough to keep me busy. I'm going to get a license to practice medicine, so if there's any sickness around I can be of some use. You say it's fifty miles to the nearest doctor. But that needn't make a grass widow necessary. I can keep house—it looks better than when I came, and you know it." Which remark would have hurt the feelings of several well-meaning cow-punchers, had they overheard it.

"Oh, I ain't finding fault with your housekeeping—you do pretty well for a green hand. But Patsy'll have to go with the round-up when it starts, and what men I keep on the ranch will have to eat with us. That's the way I've been used to fixing things; I was never so good I couldn't eat at the same table with my men; if they wasn't fit for my company I fired 'em and got fellows that was. I've had this bunch a good long while, now. You can do all right with just me, but you couldn't cook for two or three men; you can't cook good enough, even if it wasn't too much work." J. G. had a blunt way of stating disagreeable facts, occasionally.

"Very well, get your grass widow by all means," retorted she, with much wasted dignity.

"She's a swell cook, and a fine housekeeper, and she'll keep yuh from getting lonesome. She's good company, the Countess is." He grinned when he said it. "I'll have Chip ketch up the creams, and you get ready and go along with us. It'll give you a chance to size up the kind uh neighbors yuh got."

There was real pleasure in driving swiftly over

the prairie land, through the sweet, spring sunshine, and Miss Whitmore tingled with enthusiasm till they drove headlong into a deep coulee which sheltered the Denson family.

"This road is positively dangerous!" she exclaimed when they reached a particularly steep place and Chip threw all his weight upon the brake.

"We'll get the Countess in beside yuh, coming back, and then yuh won't rattle around in the seat so much. She's good and solid—just hang onto her and you'll be all right," said J. G.

"If I don't like her looks—and I know I won't—I'll get into the front seat and you can hang onto her yourself, Mr. J. G. Whitmore."

Chip, who had been silent till now, glanced briefly over his shoulder.

"It's a cinch you'll take the front seat," he remarked, laconically.

"J. G., if you hire a woman like that——"

"Like what? Doggone it, it takes a woman to jump at conclusions! The Countess is all right. She talks some——"

"I'd tell a man she does!" broke in Chip, tersely.

"Well, show me the woman that don't! Don't you be bluffed so easy, Dell. I never seen the woman yet that Chip had any time for. The Countess is all right, and she certainly can cook! I admit she talks consider'ble——"

Chip laughed grimly, and the Old Man subsided.

At the house a small, ginger-whiskered man came down to the gate to greet them.

"Why, how-de-do! I couldn't make out who 't was comin', but Mary, she up an' rek'nized the horses. Git right out an' come on in! We've had our dinner, but I guess the wimmin folks can scare ye up a bite uh suthin'. This yer sister? We heard she was up t' your place. She the one that set one uh your horse's leg? Bill, he was tellin' about it. I dunno as wimmin horse doctors is very common, but I dunno why not. I get a horse with somethin' the matter of his foot, and I dunno what. I'd like t' have ye take a look at it, fore ye go. 'Course, I expect t' pay ye."

The Old Man winked appreciatively at Chip before he came humanely to the rescue and explained that his sister was not a horse doctor, and Mr. Denson, looking very disappointed, reiterated his invitation to enter.

Mrs. Denson, a large woman who narrowly escaped being ginger-whiskered like her husband, beamed upon them from the doorway.

"Come right on in! Louise, here's comp'ny! The house is all tore up—we been tryin' t' clean house a little. Lay off yer things an' I'll git yuh some dinner right away. I'm awful glad yuh come over—I do hate t' see folks stand on cer'mony out here where neighbors is so skurce. I guess yuh think we ain't been very neighborly, but we been tryin' t' clean house, an' me an' Louise ain't had a minute we could dast call our own, er we'd a been over t' seen yuh before now. Yuh must git awful lonesome, comin' right out from the East where neighbors is thick. Do lay off yer things!"

Della looked appealingly at J. G., who again came to the rescue. Somehow he made himself heard long enough to explain their errand, and to emphasize the fact that they were in a great hurry, and had eaten dinner before they started from home. In his sister's opinion he made one exceedingly rash statement. He said that he wished to hire Mrs. Denson's sister for the summer. Mrs. Denson immediately sent a shrill call for Louise.

Then appeared the Countess, tall, gaunt and muscular, with sallow skin and a nervous manner.

"The front seat or walk!" declared Miss Whitmore, mentally, after a brief scrutiny and began storing up a scathing rebuke for J. G.

"Louise, this is Miss Whitmore," began Mrs. Denson, cheerfully, fortified by a fresh lungful of air. "They're after yuh t' go an' keep house for 'em, an' I guess yuh better go, seein' we got the house cleaned all but whitewashin' the cellar an' milk room an' kals'minin' the upstairs, an' I'll make Bill do that, an' 't won't hurt him a mite. They'll give yuh twenty-five dollars a month an' keep yuh all summer, an' as much longer as his sister stays. I guess yuh might as well go, fer they can't git anybody else that'll keep things up in shape an' be comp'ny fer his sister, an' I b'lieve in helpin' a neighbor out when yuh can. You go right an' pack up yer trunk, an' don't worry about me—I'll git along somehow, now the house-cleanin's most done."

Louise had been talking also, but her sister seemed to have a stronger pair of lungs, for her voice drowned that of the Countess, who retreated to "pack up."

The minutes dragged by, to the tune of several chapters of family history as voluminously interpreted by Mrs. Denson. Miss Whitmore had always boasted the best-behaved of nerves, but this day she developed a genuine case of "fidgets." Once she saw Chip's face turned inquiringly toward the window, and telegraphed her state of mind—while Mrs. Denson's back was turned—so eloquently that Chip was swept at once into sympathetic good-fellowship. He arranged the cushion on the front seat significantly, and was rewarded by an emphatic, though furtive, nod and smile. Whereupon he leaned comfortably back, rolled a cigarette and smoked contentedly, at peace with himself and the world—though he did not in the least know why.

"An' as I told Louise, folks has got t' put up with things an' not be huntin' trouble with a club all the time, if they expect t' git any comfort out uh this life. We ain't had the best uh luck, seems t' me, but we always git along somehow, an' we ain't had no sickness except when——"

A confused uproar arose in the room above them, followed immediately by a humpety bump and a crash as a small, pink object burst open a door and rolled precipitately into their midst. It proved to be one of the little Densons, who kicked feebly with both feet and then lay still.

"Mercy upon us! Ellen, who pushed Sary down them stairs? She's kilt!"

Della sprang up and lifted the child in her arms, passing her hand quickly over the head and plump body.

"Bring a little cold water, Mrs. Denson. She's only stunned, I think."

"Well, it does beat all how handy you go t' work.

Anybody c'd see t' you know your business. I'm awful glad you was here—there, darlin', don't cry—Ellen, an' Josephine, an' Sybilly, an' Margreet, you come down here t' me!"

The quartet, snuffling and reluctant, was dragged ignominously to the middle of the floor and there confessed, 'mid tears and much recrimination, that they had been peeping down at the "comp'ny" through various knot-holes in the chamber floor; that, as Sary's knot-hole was next the wall, her range of vision was restricted to the thin spot upon the crown of J. G.'s head, and the back of his neck. Sary longed for sight of the woman horse doctor, and when she essayed to crowd in and usurp Ellen's point of vantage, there ensued a war of extermination which ended in the literal downfall of Sary.

By the time this checked-apron court of inquiry adjourned, Louise appeared and said she believed she was ready, and Miss Whitmore escaped from the house far in advance of the others—and such were Chip's telepathic powers that he sprang down voluntarily and assisted her to the front seat without a word being said by either.

Followed a week of dullness at the ranch, with the Countess scrubbing and dusting and cleaning from morning till night. The Little Doctor, as the bunk house had christened her, was away attending the State Medical Examination at Helena.

"Gee whiz!" sighed Cal on Sunday afternoon. "It seems mighty queer without the Little Doctor around here, sassing the Old Man and putting the hull bunch of us on the fence about once a day. If it wasn't for Len Adams——"

"It wouldn't do you any good to throw a nasty loop at the Little Doctor," broke in Weary, " 'cause she's spoken for, by all signs and tokens. There's some fellow back East got a long rope on her."

"You got the papers for that?" jeered Cal. "The Little Doctor don't act the way I'd want my girl t' act, supposin' I was some thousand or fifteen hundred miles off her range. She ain't doing no pining, I tell yuh those."

"She's doing a lot of writing, though. I'll bet

money, if we called the roll right here, you'd see there's been a letter a week hittin' the trail to one Dr. Cecil Granthum, Gilroy, Ohio."

"That's what," agreed Jack Bates. "I packed one last week, myself."

"I done worse than that," said Weary, blandly. "I up and fired a shot at her, after the second one she handed me. I says, as innocent: 'I s'pose, if I lost this, there'd be a fellow out on the next train with blood in his eye and a six-gun in both hands, demanding explanations'—and she flashed them dimples on me and twinkled them big, gray eyes of hers, and says: 'It's up to you to carry it safe, then,' or words to that effect. I took notice she didn't deny but what he would."

"Two doctors in one family—gee whiz!" mused Cal. "If I hadn't got the only girl God ever made right, I'd give one Dr. Cecil Granthum, of Gilroy, Ohio, a run for his money, I tell yuh those. I'd impress it upon him that a man's taking long chances when he stands and lets his best girl stampede out here among us cow-punchers for a change uh grass.

That fellow needs looking after; he ain't finished his education. Jacky, you ain't got a female girl yanking your heart around, sail in and show us what yuh can do in that line."

"Nit," said Jack Bates, briefly. "My heart's doing business at the old stand and doing it satisfactory and proper. I don't want to set it to bucking—over a girl that wouldn't have me at any price. Let Slim. The Little Doctor's half stuck on him, anyhow."

While the boys amused themselves in serious debate with Slim, Chip put away his magazine and went down to visit Silver in the box stall. He was glad they had not attempted to draw him into the banter—they had never once thought to do so, probably, though he had been thrown into the company of the Little Doctor more than any of the others, for several good reasons. He had broken the creams to harness, and always drove them, for the Old Man found them more than he cared to tackle. And there was Silver, with frequent discussions over his progress toward recovery and some argument over his treatment—for Chip had certain ideas of his own concerning horses, and was not backward about expressing them upon occasion.

That the Little Doctor should write frequent letters to a man in the East did not concern him—why should it? Still, a fellow without a home and without some woman who cares for him, cannot escape having his loneliness thrust upon him at times. He wondered why he should care. Surely, ten years of living his life alone ought to kill that latent homesickness which used to hold him awake at nights. Sometimes even of late years, when he stood guard over the cattle at night, and got to thinking—oh, it was hell to be all alone in the world!

There were Cal and Weary, they had girls who loved them—and they were sure welcome to them. And Jack Bates and Happy Jack had sisters and mothers—and even Slim had an old maid aunt who always knit him a red and green pair of wristlets for Christmas. Chip, smoothing mechanically the shimmery, white mane of his pet, thought he might be contented if he had even an old maid aunt—but he would see that she made his wristlets of some other color than those bestowed every year upon Slim.

As for the Little Doctor, it would be something strange if she had gone through life without having some fellow in love with her. Probably, if the truth was known, there had been more than Dr. Cecil Granthum—bah, what a sickening name! Cecil! It might as well be Adolphus or Regie or—what does a man want to pack around a name like that for? Probably he was the kind of man that the name sounded like; a dude with pink cheeks.

Chip knew just how he looked. Inspiration suddenly seizing upon him, he sat down upon the manger, drew his memorandum book out of his inner coat pocket, carefully sharpened a bit of lead pencil which he found in another pocket, tore a leaf from the book, and, with Silver looking over his shoulder, drew a graphic, ideal picture of Dr. Cecil Granthum.

CHAPTER V.

In Silver's Stall.

"Oh, are *you* here? It's a wonder you don't have your bed brought down here, so you can sleep near Silver. How has he been doing since I left?"

Chip simply sat still upon the edge of the manger and stared. His gray hat was pushed far back upon his head and his dark hair waved and curled upon his forehead, very much as a girl's might have done. He did not know that he was a very good-looking young man, but perhaps the Little Doctor did. She smiled and came up and patted Silver, who had forgotten that he ever had objected to her nearness. He nickered a soft welcome and laid his nose on her shoulder.

"You've been drawing a picture. Who's the victim of your satirical pencil this time?" The Little Doctor, reaching out quickly, calmly appropriated the sketch before Chip had time to withdraw it, even if he had cared to do so. He was busy wondering how the Little Doctor came to be there at that particular time, and had forgotten the picture, which he had not quite finished labeling.

"Dr. Cecil——" Miss Whitmore turned red at first, then broke into laughter. "Oh-h, ha! ha! ha! Silver, you don't know how funny this master of yours can be! Ha! ha!" She raised her head from Silver's neck, where it had rested, and wiped her eyes.

"How did you know about Cecil?" she demanded of a very discomfited young man upon the manger.

"I didn't know—and I didn't *want* to know. I heard the boys talking and joshing about him, and I just drew—their own conclusions." Chip grinned a little and whittled at his pencil, and wondered how much of the statement was a lie.

Miss Whitmore turned red again, and ended by laughing even more heartily than at first.

"Their conclusions aren't very complimentary," she said. "I don't believe Dr. Cecil would feel flattered at this. Why those bowed legs, may I ask, and wherefore that long, lean, dyspeptic visage? Dr. Cecil, let me inform you, has a digestion that quails not at deviled crabs and chafing-dish horrors at midnight, as I have abundant reason to know. I have seen Dr. Cecil prepare a welsh rabbit and—eat it, also, with much relish, apparently. Oh, no, their conclusions weren't quite correct. There are other details I might mention—that cane, for instance—but let it pass. I shall keep this, I think, as a companion to 'The old maid's credential card.' "

"Are you in the habit of keeping other folk's property?" inquired Chip, with some acerbity.

"Nothing but personal caricatures—and hearts, perhaps," returned the Little Doctor, sweetly.

"I hardly think your collection of the last named article is very large," retorted Chip.

"Still, I added to the collection to-day," pursued Miss Whitmore, calmly. "I shared my seat in the train with J. G.'s silent partner (I did not find him silent, however), Mr. Duncan Whitaker. He hired a team in Dry Lake and we came out together, and

I believe—please don't mention Dr. Cecil Granthum to him, will you?"

Chip wished, quite savagely, that she wouldn't let those dimples dodge into her cheeks, and the laugh dodge into her eyes, like that. It made a fellow uncomfortable. He was thoroughly disgusted with her—or he would be, if she would only stop looking like that. He was in that state of mind where his only salvation, seemingly, lay in quarreling with some one immediately.

"So old Dunk's come back? If you've got his heart, you must have gone hunting it with a microscope, for it's a mighty small one—almost as small as his soul. No one else even knew he had one. You ought to have it set in a ring, so you won't lose it."

"I don't wear phony jewelry, thank you," said Miss Whitmore, and Chip thought dimples weren't so bad, after all.

The Little Doctor was weaving Silver's mane about her white fingers and meditating deeply. Chip wondered if she were thinking of Dr. Cecil.

"Where did you learn to draw like that?" she asked, suddenly, turning toward him. "You do much better than I, and I've always been learning from good teachers. Did you ever try painting?"

Chip blushed and looked away from her. This was treading close to his deep-hidden, inner self.

"I don't know where I learned. I never took a lesson in my life, except from watching people and horses and the country, and remembering the lines they made, you know. I always made pictures, ever since I can remember—but I never tried colors very much. I never had a chance, working around cow-camps and on ranches."

"I'd like to have you look over some of my sketches and things—and I've paints and canvas, if you ever care to try that. Come up to the house some evening and I'll show you my daubs. They're none of them as good as 'The Old Maid.' "

"I wish you'd tear that thing up!" said Chip, vehemently.

"Why? The likeness is perfect. One would think you were designer for a fashion paper, the way you got the tucks in my sleeve and the braid on my collar—and you might have had the kindness to *tell* me my hat was on crooked, I think!"

There was a rustle in the loose straw, a distant slam of the stable door, and Chip sat alone with his horse, whittling abstractedly at his pencil till his knife blade grated upon the metal which held the eraser.

CHAPTER VI.

The Hum of Preparation.

Miss Whitmore ran down to the blacksmith shop, waving an official-looking paper in her hand.

"I've got it, J. G.!"

"Got what—smallpox?" J. G. did not even look up from the iron he was welding.

"No, my license. I'm a really, truly doctor now, and you needn't laugh, either. You said you'd give a dance if I passed, and I did. Happy Jack brought it just now."

"Brought the dance?" The Old Man gave the bellows a pull which sent a shower of sparks toward the really, truly doctor.

"Brought the license," she explained, patiently. "You can see for yourself. They were awfully nice to me—they seemed to think a girl doctor is some kind of joke out here. They didn't make it any easier, though; they acted as if they didn't expect me to pass—but I did!"

The Old Man rubbed one smutty hand down his trousers leg and extended it for the precious document. "Let me have a look at it," he said, trying to hide his pride in her.

"Well, but I'll hold it. Your hands are dirty." Dr. Whitmore eyed the hands disapprovingly.

The Old Man read it slowly through, growing prouder every line.

"You're all right, Dell—I'll be doggoned if you ain't. Don't you worry about the dance—I'll see't yuh get it. You go tell the Countess to bake up a lot of cake and truck, and I'll send some uh the boys around t' tell the neighbors. Better have it Friday night, I guess—I'm goin t' start the round-up out early next week. Doggone it! I've gone and burned that weldin'. Go on and stop your botherin' me!"

In two minutes the Little Doctor was back, breathless.

"What about the music, J. G.? We want *good* music."

"Well, I'll tend t' that part. Say! You can rig up that room off the dining room for your office—I s'pose you'll have to have one. You make out a list of what dope you want—and be sure yuh get a-plenty. I look for an unhealthy summer among the cow-punchers. If I ain't mistook in the symptoms, Dunk's got palpitation uh the heart right now—an' got it serious."

The Old Man chuckled to himself and went back to his welding.

"Oh, Louise!" The Little Doctor hurried to where the Countess was scrubbing the kitchen steps with soft soap and sand and considerable energy. "J. G. says I may have a dance next Friday night, so we must hurry and fix the house—only I don't see much fixing to be done; everything is *so* clean."

"Oh, there ain't a room in the house fit fer comp'ny t' walk into," expostulated the Countess while she scrubbed. "I do like t' see a house clean when folks is expected that only come t' be critical an' make remarks behind yer back the minit they git away. If folks got anything t' say I'd a good deal ruther they said it t' my face an' be done with it. 'Yuh can know a man's face but yuh can't know his heart,' as the sayin' is, an' it's the same way with women—anyway, it's the same way with Mis' Beckman. You can know her face a mile off, but yuh never know who she's goin' t' rake over the coals next. As the sayin' is: 'The tongue of a woman, at last it biteth like a serpent an' it stingeth like an addle,' an' I guess it's so. Anyway, Mis' Beckman's does. I do b'lieve on my soul—what's the matter, Dell? What yuh laughin' at?"

The Little Doctor was past speech for the moment, and the Countess stood up and looked curiously around her. It never occurred to her that she might be the cause of that convulsive outburst.

"Oh—he—never mind—he's gone, now."

"Who's gone?" persisted the Countess.

"What kinds of cake do you think we ought to have?" asked the Little Doctor, diplomatically.

The Countess sank to her knees and dipped a handful of amber, jelly-like soap from a tin butter can.

"Well, I don't know. I s'pose folks will look for something fancy, seein' you're givin' the dance. Mis' Beckman sets herself up as a shinin' example on cake, and she'll come just t' be critical an' find fault, if she can. If I can't bake all around her the best day she ever seen, I'll give up cookin' anything but spuds. She had the soggiest kind uh jelly roll t' the su'prise on Mary last winter. I know it was hern, fer I seen her bring it in, an' I went straight an' ondone it. I guess it was kinda mean uh me, but I don't care—as the sayin' is: 'What's sass fer the goose is good enough sass fer anybody'—an' she done the same trick by me, at the su'prise at Adamses last fall. But she couldn't find no kick about *my* cake, an' hers—yuh c'd of knocked a cow down with it left-handed! If that's the best she c'n do on cake I'd advise 'er to keep the next batch t' home where they're used to it. They say't 'What's one man's meat 's pizen t' the other feller,' and I guess it's so enough. Maybe Mame an' the rest uh them Beckman kids can eat sech truck without comin' down in a bunch with gastakutus, but I'd hate t' tackle it myself."

The Little Doctor gurgled. This was a malady which had not been mentioned at the medical college.

"Where shall we set the tables, if we dance in the dining room?" she asked, having heard enough of the Beckmans for the present.

"Why, we won't set any tables. Folks always have a lap supper at ranch dances. At the su'prise on Mary——"

"What is a lap supper?"

"Well, my stars alive! Where under the shinin' sun was you brought up if yuh never heard of a lap supper? A lap supper is where folks set around the walls—or any place they can find—and take the plates on their laps and yuh pass 'em stuff. The san'wiches——"

"You do make such beautiful bread!" interrupted the Little Doctor, very sincerely.

"Well, I ain't had the best uh luck, lately, but I

guess it does taste good after that bread yuh had when I come. Soggy was no name for——"

"Patsy made that bread," interposed Miss Whitmore, hastily. "He had bad luck, and——"

"I guess he did!" sniffed the Countess, contemptuously. "As I told Mary when I come——"

"I wonder how many cakes we'll need?" Miss Whitmore, you will observe, had learned to interrupt when she had anything to say. It was the only course to pursue with anyone from Denson coulee.

The Countess, having finished her scrubbing, rose jerkily and upset the soap can, which rolled over and over down the steps, leaving a yellow trail as it went.

"Well, there, if that wasn't a bright trick uh mine! They say the more yuh hurry the less yuh'll git along, an' that's a sample. We'd ought t' have five kinds, an' about four uh each kind. It wouldn't do t' run out, er Mis' Beckman never would let anybody hear the last of it. Down t' Mary's——"

"Twenty cakes! Good gracious! I'll have to

order my stock of medicine, for I'll surely have a houseful of patients if the guests eat twenty cakes."

"Well, as the sayin' is: 'Patience an' perseverance can git away with most anything,' " observed the Countess, naïvely.

The Little Doctor retired behind her handkerchief.

"My stars alive, I do b'lieve my bread's beginnin' t' scorch!" cried the Countess, and ran to see. The Little Doctor followed her inside and sat down.

"We must make a list of the things we'll need, Louise. You——"

"Dell! Oh-h, Dell!" The voice of the Old Man resounded from the parlor.

"I'm in the kitchen!" called she, remaining where she was. He tramped heavily through the house to her.

"I'll send the rig in, t'morrow, if there's anything yuh want," he remarked. "And if you'll make out a list uh dope, I'll send the order in t' the Falls. We've got plenty uh saws an' cold chisels down in the blacksmith shop—you can pick out what yuh want." He dodged and grinned. "Got any cake, Countess?"

"Well, there ain't a thing cooked, hardly. I'm going t' bake up something right after dinner. Here's some sponge cake—but it ain't fit t' eat, hardly. I let Dell look in the oven, 'cause my han's was all over flour, an' she slammed the door an' it fell. But yuh can't expect one person t' know everything—an' too many han's can't make decent soup, as the sayin' is, an' it's the same way with cake."

The Old Man winked at the Little Doctor over a great wedge of feathery delight. "I don't see nothing the matter with this—only it goes down too easy," he assured the Countess between mouthfuls. "Fix up your list, Dell, and don't be afraid t' order everything yuh need. I'll foot the——"

The Old Man, thinking to go back to his work, stepped into the puddle of soft soap and sat emphatically down upon the top step, coasting rapidly to the bottom. A carpet slipper shot through the open door and landed in the dishpan; the other slipper disappeared mysteriously. The wedge of cake was immediately pounced upon by an investigative hen and carried in triumph to her brood.

"Good Lord!" J. G. struggled painfully to his feet. "Dell, who in thunder put that stuff there? You're a little too doggoned anxious for somebody t' practice on, seems t' me." A tiny trickle of blood showed in the thin spot on his head.

"Are you hurt, J. G.? We—I spilled the soap." The Little Doctor gazed solicitous, from the doorway.

"Huh! I see yuh spilled the soap, all right enough. I'm willin' to believe yuh did without no affidavit. Doggone it, a bachelor never has any such a man-trap around in a fellow's road. I've lived in Montana fourteen years, an' I never slipped up on my own doorstep till you got here. It takes a woman t' leave things around—where's my cake?"

"Old Specle took it down by the bunk house. Shall I go after it?"

"No, you needn't. Doggone it, this wading through ponds uh soft soap has got t' stop right here. I never had t' do it when I was baching, I notice."

He essayed, with the aid of a large splinter, to scrape the offending soap from his trousers.

"Certainly, you didn't. Bachelors never use soap," retorted Della.

"Oh, they don't, hey? That's all you know about it. They don't use this doggoned, slimy truck, let me tell yuh. What d'yuh want, Chip? Oh, you've got t' grin, too! Dell, why don't yuh do something fer my head? What's your license good fer, I'd like t' know? You didn't see Dell's license, did yuh, Chip? Go and get it an' show it to him, Dell. It's good fer everything but gitting married —there ain't any cure for that complaint."

CHAPTER VII.

Love and a Stomach Pump.

An electrical undercurrent of expectation pervaded the very atmosphere of Flying U ranch. The musicians, two supercilious but undeniably efficient young men from Great Falls, had arrived two hours before and were being graciously entertained by the Little Doctor up at the house. The sandwiches stood waiting, the coffee was ready for the boiling water, and the dining-room floor was smooth as wax could make it.

For some reason unknown to himself, Chip was "in the deeps." He even threatened to stop in the bunk house and said he didn't feel like dancing, but was brought into line by weight of numbers. He hated Dick Brown, anyway, for his cute, little yellow mustache that curled up at the ends like the tail of a drake. He had snubbed him all the way out from town and handled Dick's guitar with a recklessness that invited disaster. And the way Dick smirked when the Old Man introduced him to the Little Doctor—a girl with a fellow in the East oughtn't to let her eyes smile that way at a pin-headed little dude like Dick Brown, anyway. And he—Chip—had given her a letter postmarked blatantly: "Gilroy, Ohio, 10:30 P. M."—and she had been so taken up with those cussed musicians that she couldn't even thank him, and only just glanced at the letter before she stuck it inside her belt. Probably she wouldn't even read it till after the dance. He wondered if Dr. Cecil Granthum cared—oh, hell! Of *course* he cared—that is, if he had any sense at all. But the Little Doctor—she wasn't above flirting, he noticed. If *he* ever fell in love with a girl—which the Lord forbid—he'd take mighty good care she didn't get time to make dimples and smiles for some other fellow to go to heaven looking at.

There, that was her, laughing like she always laughed—it reminded him of pines nodding in a canyon and looking wise and whispering things they'd seen and heard before you were born, and of water falling over rocks, somehow. Queer, maybe —but it did. He wondered if Dick Brown had been trying to say something funny. He didn't see, for the life of him, how the Little Doctor could laugh at that little imitation man. Girls are—well, they're easy pleased, most of them.

Down in the bunk house the boys were hurrying into their "war togs"—which is, being interpreted, their best clothes. There was a nervous scramble over the cracked piece of a bar mirror—which had a history—and cries of "Get out!" "Let me there a minute, can't yuh?" and "Get up off my coat!" were painfully frequent.

Happy Jack struggled blindly with a refractory red tie, which his face rivaled in hue and sheen—for he had been generous of soap.

Weary had possessed himself of the glass and was shaving as leisurely as though four restive cow-punchers were not waiting anxiously their turn.

"For the Lord's sake, Weary!" spluttered Jack Bates. "Your whiskers grow faster'n you can shave 'em off, at that gait. Get a move on, can't yuh?"

Weary turned his belathered face sweetly upon Jack. "Getting in a hurry, Jacky? *Your* girl won't be there, and nobody else's girl is going to have time to see whether you shaved to-day or last Christmas. You don't want to worry so much about your looks, none of you. I hate to say it, but you act vain, all of you kids. Honest, I'm ashamed. Look at that gaudy countenance Happy's got on—and his necktie's most as bad." He stropped his razor with exasperating nicety, stopping now and then to test its edge upon a hair from his own brown head.

Happy Jack, grown desperate over his tie and purple over Weary's remarks, craned his neck over the shoulder of that gentleman and leered into the mirror. When Happy liked, he could contort his naturally plain features into a diabolical grin which sent prickly waves creeping along the spine of the beholder.

Weary looked, stared, half rose from his chair.

"Holy smithereens! Quit it, Happy! You look like the devil by lightning."

Happy, watching, seized the hand that held the

razor; Cal, like a cat, pounced upon the mirror, and Jack Bates deftly wrenched the razor from Weary's fingers.

"Whoopee, boys! Some of you tie Weary down and set on him while I shave," cried Cal, jubilant over the mutiny. "We'll make short work of this toilet business."

Whereupon Weary was borne to the floor, bound hand and foot with silk handkerchiefs, carried bodily and laid upon his bed.

"Oh, the things I won't do to you for this!" he asserted, darkly. "There won't nary a son-of-a-gun uh yuh get a dance from my little schoolma'am—you'll see!" He grinned prophetically, closed his eyes and murmured: "Call me early, mother dear," and straightway fell away into slumber and peaceful snoring, while the lather dried upon his face.

"Better turn Weary loose and wake him up, Chip," suggested Jack Bates, half an hour later, shoving the stopper into his cologne bottle and making for the door. "At the rate the rigs are rolling in, it'll take us all to put up the teams." The door slammed behind him as it had done behind the others as they hurried away.

"Here!" Chip untied Weary's hands and feet and took him by the shoulder. "Wake up, Willie, if you want to be Queen o' the May."

Weary sat up and rubbed his eyes. "Confound them two Jacks! What time is it?"

"A little after eight. *Your* crowd hasn't come yet, so you needn't worry. I'm not going up yet for a while, myself."

"You're off your feed. Brace up and take all there is going, my son." Weary prepared to finish his interrupted beautification.

"I'm going to—all the bottles, that is. If that Dry Lake gang comes loaded down with whisky, like they generally do, we ought to get hold of it and cache every drop, Weary."

Weary turned clear around to stare his astonishment.

"When did the W. C. T. U. get you by the collar?" he demanded.

"Aw, don't be a fool, Weary," retorted Chip.

"You can see it wouldn't look right for us to let any of the boys get full, or even half shot, seeing this is the Little Doctor's dance."

Weary meditatively scraped his left jaw and wiped the lather from the razor upon a fragment of newspaper.

"Splinter, we've throwed in together ever since we drifted onto the same range, and I'm with you, uh course. But—don't overlook Dr. Cecil Granthum. I'd hate like the devil to see you git throwed down, because it'd hurt you worse than anybody I know."

Chip calmly sifted some tobacco into a cigarette paper. His mouth was very straight and his brows very close together.

"It's a devilish good thing it was *you* said that, Weary. If it had been anyone else I'd punch his face for him."

"Why, yes—an' I'd help you, too." Weary, his mouth very much on one side of his face that he might the easier shave the other, spoke in fragments. "You don't take it amiss from—me, though. I can see——"

The door slammed with extreme violence, and Weary slashed his chin unbecomingly in consequence, but he felt no resentment toward Chip. He calmly stuck a bit of paper on the cut to stop the bleeding and continued to shave.

A short time after, the Little Doctor came across Chip glaring at Dick Brown, who was strumming his guitar with ostentatious ease upon an inverted dry-goods box at one end of the long dining room.

"I came to ask a favor of you," she said, "but my courage oozed at the first glance."

"It's hard to believe your courage would ooze at anything. What's the favor?"

The Little Doctor bent her head and lowered her voice to a confidential undertone which caught at Chip's blood and set it leaping.

"I want you to come and help me turn my drug store around with its face to the wall. All the later editions of Denson, Pilgreen and Beckman have taken possession of my office—and as the Countess says: 'Them Beckman kids is holy terrors—an' it's savin' the rod an' spoilin' the kid that makes 'em so!' "

Chip laughed outright. "The Denson kids are a heap worse, if she only knew it," he said, and followed her willingly.

The Little Doctor's "office" was a homey little room, with a couch, a well-worn Morris rocker, two willow chairs and a small table for the not imposing furnishing, dignified by a formidable stack of medical books in one corner, and the "drug store," which was simply a roomy bookcase filled with jars, bottles, boxes and packages, all labeled in a neat vertical hand.

The room fairly swarmed with children, who seemed, for the most part, to be enjoying themselves very much. Charlotte May Pilgreen and Sary Denson were hunched amicably over one of the books, shuddering beatifically over a pictured skeleton. A swarm surrounded the drug store, the glass door of which stood open.

The Little Doctor flew across to the group, horror white.

"Sybilly got the key an' unlocked it, an' she give us this candy, too!" tattled a Pilgreen with very red hair and a very snub nose.

"I didn't, either! It was Jos'phine!"

"Aw, you big story-teller! I never tetched it!"

The Little Doctor clutched the nearest arm till the owner of it squealed.

"How many of you have eaten some of these? Tell the truth, now." They quailed before her sternness—quailed and confessed. All told, seven had swallowed the sweet pellets, in numbers ranging from two to a dozen more.

"Is it poison?" Chip whispered the question in the ear of the perturbed Little Doctor.

"No—but it will make them exceedingly uncomfortable for a time—I'm going to pump them out."

"Good shot! Serves 'em right, the little——"

"All of you who have eaten this—er—candy, must come with me. The rest of you may stay here and play, but you must *not* touch this case."

"Yuh going t' give 'em a lickin'?" Sary Denson wetted a finger copiously before turning a leaf upon the beautiful skeleton.

"Never mind what I'm going to do to them—you had better keep out of mischief yourself, however. Mr. Bennett, I wish you would get some fellow you can trust—some one who won't talk about this afterward—turn this case around so that it will be safe, and then come to the back bedroom—the one off the kitchen. And tell Louise I want her, will you, please?"

"I'll get old Weary. Yes, I'll send the Countess—but don't you think she's a mighty poor hand to keep a secret?"

"I can't help it—I need her. Hurry, please."

Awed by the look in her big, gray eyes and the mysterious summoning of help, the luckless seven were marched silently through the outer door, around the house, through the coal shed and so into the back bedroom, without being observed by the merrymakers, who shook the house to its foundation to the cheerful command: "Gran' right 'n' left with a double *elbow-w!*" "Chasse by yer pardner—balance—*swing!*"

"What under the shinin' sun's the matter, Dell?" The Countess, breathless from dancing, burst in upon the little group.

"Nothing very serious, Louise, though it's rather uncomfortable to be called from dancing to administer heroic remedies by wholesale. Can you hold Josephine—whichever one that is? She ate the most, as nearly as I can find out."

"She ain't gone an' took pizen, has she? What was it—strychnine? I'll bet them Beckman kids put 'er up to it. Yuh goin' t' give 'er an anticdote?"

"I'm going to use this." The Little Doctor held up a fearsome thing to view. "Open your mouth, Josephine."

Josephine refused; her refusal was emphatic and unequivocal, punctuated by sundry kicks directed at whoever came within range of her stout little shoes.

"It ain't no use t' call Mary in—Mary can't handle her no better'n I can—an' not so good. Jos'phine, yuh got——"

"Here's where we shine," broke in a cheery voice which was sweet to the ears, just then. "Chip and I ain't wrassled with bronks all our lives for nothing. This is dead easy—all same branding calves. Ketch hold of her heels, Splinter—that's the talk. Countess, you better set your back against that door—some of these dogies is thinking of taking a sneak on us—and we'd have t' go some, to cut 'em out uh that bunch out there and corral 'em again. There yuh are, Doctor—sail in."

Upheld mentally by the unfailing sunniness of Weary and the calm determination of Chip, to whom flying heels and squirming bodies were as nothing, or at most a mere trifle, the Little Doctor set to work with a thoroughness and dispatch which struck terror to the hearts of the guilty seven.

It did not take long—as Weary had said, it was very much like branding calves. No sooner was one child made to disgorge and laid, limp and subdued, upon the bed, than Chip and Weary seized another dexterously by heels and head. The Countess did nothing beyond guarding the door and acting as chaperon to the undaunted Little Doctor; but she did her duty and held her tongue afterward—which was a great deal for her to do.

The Little Doctor sat down in a chair, when it was all over, looking rather white. Chip moved nearer, though there was really nothing that he could do beyond handing her a glass of water, which she accepted gratefully.

Weary held a little paper trough of tobacco in his fingers and drew the tobacco sack shut with his teeth. His eyes were fixed reflectively upon the bed. He placed the sack absently in his pocket, still meditating other things.

" 'She answered: "We are seven," ' " he quoted softly and solemnly, and the Little Doctor forgot her faintness in a hearty laugh.

"You two go back to your dancing now," she commanded, letting the dimples stand in her cheeks in a way that Chip dreamed about afterward. "I don't know what I should have done without you—

a cow-puncher seems born to meet emergencies in just the right way. *Please* don't tell anyone, will you?"

"Never. Don't you worry about us, Doctor. Chip and I don't set up nights emptying our brains out our mouths. We don't tell our secrets to nobody but our horses—and they're dead safe."

"You needn't think I'll tell, either," said the Countess, earnestly. "I ain't forgot how you took the blame uh that sof' soap, Dell. As the sayin' is——"

Weary closed the door then, so they did not hear the saying which seemed to apply to this particular case. His arm hooked into Chip's, he led the way through the kitchen and down the hill to the hay corral. Once safe from observation, he threw himself into the sweetly pungent "blue-joint" and laughed and laughed.

Chip's nervous system did not demand the relief of cachinnation. He went away to Silver's stall and groped blindly to the place where two luminous, green moons shone upon him in the darkness. He rubbed the delicate nose gently and tangled his fingers in the dimly gleaming mane, as he had seen *her* do. Such pink little fingers they were! He laid his brown cheek against the place where he remembered them to have rested.

"Silver horse," he whispered, "if I ever fall in love with a girl—which isn't likely!—I'll want her to have dimples and big, gray eyes and a laugh like——"

CHAPTER VIII.

Prescriptions.

It was Sunday, the second day after the dance. The boys were scattered, for the day was delicious —one of those sweet, soft days which come to us early in May. Down in the blacksmith shop Chip was putting new rowels into his spurs and whistling softly to himself while he worked.

The Little Doctor had gone with him to visit Silver that morning, and had not hurried away, but had leaned against the manger and listened while he told her of the time Silver, swimming the river when it was "up," had followed him to the Shonkin camp when Chip had thought to leave him at home. And they had laughed together over the juvenile seven and the subsequent indignation of the mothers who, with the exception of "Mary," had bundled up their offspring and gone home mad. True, they had none of them thoroughly understood the situation, having only the version of the children, who accused the Little Doctor of trying to make them eat rubber —"just cause she was mad about some little old candy." The mystification of the others among the Happy Family, who scented a secret with a joke to it but despaired of wringing the truth from either Weary or Chip, was dwelt upon with much enjoyment by the Little Doctor.

It was a good old world and a pleasant, and Chip had no present quarrel with fate—or with anybody else. That was why he whistled.

Then voices reached him through the open door, and a laugh—*her* laugh. Chip smiled sympathetically, though he had not the faintest notion of the cause of her mirth. As the voices drew nearer, the soft, smooth, hated tones of Dunk Whitaker untangled from the Little Doctor's laugh, and Chip stopped whistling. Dunk was making a good, long stay of it this time; usually he came one day and went the next, and no one grieved at his departure.

"You find them an entirely new species, of course. How do you get on with them?" said Dunk.

And the Little Doctor answered him frankly and distinctly: "Oh, very well, considering all things. They furnish me with some amusement, and I give them something quite new to talk about, so we are quits. They are a good-hearted lot, you know —but *so* ignorant! I don't suppose——"

The words trailed into an indistinct murmur, punctuated by Dunk's jarring cackle.

Chip did not resume his whistling, though he might have done so if he had heard a little more, or a little less. As a matter of fact, it was the Densons, and the Pilgreens, and the Beckmans that were under discussion, and not the Flying U cowboys, as Chip believed. He no longer smiled sympathetically.

"We furnish her with some amusement, do we? That's good! We're a good-hearted lot, but *so* ignorant! The devil we are!" He struck the rivet such a blow that he snapped one shank of his spur short off. This meant ten or twelve dollars for a new pair—though the cost of it troubled him little, just then. It was something tangible upon which to pour profanity, however, and the atmosphere grew sulphurous in the vicinity of the blacksmith shop and remained so for several minutes, after which a tall, irate cow-puncher with his hat pulled low over angry eyes left the shop and strode up the path to the deserted bunk house.

He did not emerge till the Old Man called to him to ride down to Denson's after one of the Flying U horses which had broken out of the pasture.

Della was looking from the window when Chip rode up the hill upon the "coulee trail," which passed close by the house. She was tired of the platitudes of Dunk, who, trying to be both original and polished, fell far short of being either and only succeeded in being extremely tiresome.

"Where's Chip going, J. G.?" she demanded, in a proprietary tone.

"Down t' Denson's after a horse." J. G. spoke lazily, without taking his pipe from his mouth.

"Oh, I wish I could go—I wonder if he'd care." The Little Doctor spoke impulsively as was her habit.

" 'Course he wouldn't. Hey, Chip! Hold on a minute!" The Old Man stood waving his pipe in the doorway.

Chip jerked his horse to a stand-still and half turned in the saddle.

"What?"

"Dell wants t' go along. Will yuh saddle up Concho for 'er? There's no hurry, anyhow, you've got plenty uh time. Dell's afraid one uh the kids might fall downstairs ag'in, and she'd miss the case."

"I'm not, either," said the Little Doctor, coming to stand by her brother; "it's too nice a day to stay inside, and my muscles ache for a gallop over the hills."

Chip did not look up at her; he did not dare. He felt that, if he met her eyes—with the laugh in them—he should do one of two undesirable things: he should either smile back at her, weakly overlooking the hypocrisy of her friendliness, or sneer in answer to her smile, which would be very rude and ungentlemanly.

"If you had mentioned wanting a ride I should have been glad to accompany you," remarked Dunk, reproachfully, when Chip had ridden, somewhat sullenly, back to the stable.

"I didn't think of it before—thank you," said the Little Doctor, lightly, and hurried away to put on her blue riding habit with its cunning little jockey cap which she found the only headgear that would stay upon her head in the teeth of Montana wind, and which made her look—well, kissable. She was standing on the porch drawing on her gauntlets when Chip returned, leading Concho by the bridle.

"Let me help you," begged Dunk, at her elbow, hoping till the last that she would invite him to go with them.

The Little Doctor, not averse to hiding the bitter of her medicine under a coating of sugar, smiled sweetly upon him, to the delectation of Dunk and the added bitterness of Chip, who was rapidly nearing that state of mind which is locally described as being "strictly on the fight."

"I expect she thinks I'll amuse her some more!" he thought, savagely, as they galloped away through the quivering sunlight.

For the first two miles the road was level, and Chip set the pace—which was, as he intended it should be, too swift for much speech. After that the trail climbed abruptly out of Flying U coulee, and the horses were compelled to walk. Then it was that Chip's native chivalry and self-mastery were put to test.

He was hungry for a solitary ride such as had, before now, drawn much of the lonely ache out of his heart and keyed him up to the life which he must live and which chafed his spirit more than even he realized. Instead of such slender comfort, he was forced to ride beside the girl who had hurt him—so close that his knee sometimes brushed her horse—and to listen to her friendly chatter and make answer, at times, with at least some show of civility.

She was talking reminiscently of the dance.

"J. G. showed splendid judgment in his choice of musicians, didn't he?"

Chip looked straight ahead. This was touching a sore place in his memory. A vision of Dick Brown's vapid smile and curled up mustache rose before him.

"I'd tell a man," he said, with faint irony.

The Little Doctor gave him a quick, surprised look and went on.

"I liked their playing so much. Mr. Brown was especially good upon the guitar."

"Y-e-s?"

"Yes, of course. You know yourself, he plays beautifully."

"Cow-punchers aren't expected to know all these things." Chip hated himself for replying so, but the temptation mastered him.

"Aren't they? I can't see why not."

Chip closed his lips tightly to keep in something impolite.

The Little Doctor, puzzled as well as piqued, went straight to the point.

"Why didn't you like Mr. Brown's playing?"

"Did I say I didn't like it?"

"Well, you—not exactly, but you implied that you did not."

"Y-e-s?"

The Little Doctor gave the reins an impatient twitch.

"Yes, yes—*yes!*"

No answer from Chip. He could think of nothing to say that was not more or less profane.

"I think he's a very nice, amiable young man"—strong emphasis upon the second adjective. "I like amiable young men."

Silence.

"He's going to come down here hunting next fall. J. G. invited him."

"Yes? What does he expect to find?"

"Why, whatever there is to hunt. Chickens and —er—deer——"

"Exactly."

By this they reached the level and the horses

broke, of their own accord, into a gallop which somewhat relieved the strain upon the mental atmosphere. At the next hill the Little Doctor looked her companion over critically.

"Mr. Bennett, you look positively bilious. Shall I prescribe for you?"

"I can't see how that would add to your amusement."

"I'm not trying to add to my amusement."

"No?"

"If I were, there's no material at hand. Bad-tempered young men are never amusing, to me. I like——"

"Amiable young men. Such as Dick Brown."

"I think you need a change of air, Mr. Bennett."

"Yes? I've felt, lately, that Eastern airs don't agree with my constitution."

Miss Whitmore grew red as to cheeks and bright as to eyes.

"I think a few small doses of Eastern manners would improve you very much," she said, pointedly.

"Y-e-s? They'd have to be small, because the supply is very limited."

The Little Doctor grew white around the mouth. She held Concho's rein so tight he almost stopped.

"If you didn't want me to come, why in the world didn't you have the courage to say so at the start? I must say I don't admire people whose tempers—and manners—are so unstable. I'm sorry I forced my presence upon you, and I promise you it won't occur again." She hesitated, and then fired a parting shot which certainly was spiteful in the extreme. "There's one good thing about it," she smiled, tartly, "I shall have something interesting to write to Dr. Cecil."

With that she turned astonished Concho short around in the trail—and as Chip gave Blazes a vicious jab with his spurs at the same instant, the distance between them widened rapidly.

As Chip raced away over the prairie, he discovered a new and puzzling kink in his temper. He had been angry with the Little Doctor for coming, but it was nothing to the rage he felt when she turned back! He did not own to himself that he wanted her beside him to taunt and to hurt with his rudeness, but it was a fact, for all that. And it was a very surly young man who rode into the Denson corral and threw a loop over the head of the runaway.

CHAPTER IX.

Before the Round-up.

"The Little Doctor wants us all to come up t' the White House this evening and have some music," announced Cal, bursting into the bunk house where the boys were sorting and packing their belongings ready to start with the round-up wagon in the morning.

Jack Bates hurriedly stuffed a miscellaneous collection of socks and handkerchiefs into his war bag and made for the wash basin.

"I'll just call her bluff," he said, determinedly.

"It ain't any bluff; she wants us t' come, er you bet she wouldn't say so. I've learned that much about her. Say, you'd a died to seen old Dunk look down his nose! I'll bet money she done it just t' rasp his feelin's—and she sure succeeded. I'd go anyway, now, just t' watch him squirm."

"I notice it grinds him consider'ble to see the

Little Doctor treat us fellows like white folks. He's workin' for a stand-in there himself. I bet he gets throwed down good and hard," commented Weary, cheerfully.

"It's a cinch he don't know about that pill-thrower back in Ohio," added Cal. "Any of you fellows going to take her bid? I'll go alone, in a minute."

"I don't think you'll go alone," asserted Jack Bates, grabbing his hat.

Slim made a few hasty passes at his hair and said he was ready. Shorty, who had just come in from riding, unbuckled his spurs and kicked them under his bed.

"It'll be many a day b'fore we listen t' the Little Doctor's mandolin ag'in," croaked Happy Jack.

"Aw, shut up!" admonished Cal.

"Come on, Chip," sang out Weary. "You can spoil good paper when you can't do anything else. Come and size up the look on Dunk's face when we take possession of all the best chairs and get t' pouring our incense and admiration on the Little Doctor."

Chip took the cigarette from his lips and emptied his lungs of smoke. "You fellows go on. I'm not going." He bent again to his eternal drawing.

"The dickens you ain't!" Weary was too astounded to say more.

Chip said nothing. His gray hat-brim shielded his face from view, save for the thin, curved lips and firm chin. Weary studied chin and lips curiously, and whatever he read there, he refrained from further argument. He knew Chip so much better than did anyone else.

"Aw, what's the matter with yuh, Splinter! Come on; don't be a chump," cried Cal, from the doorway.

"I guess you'll let a fellow do as he likes about it, won't you?" queried Chip, without looking up. He was very busy, just then, shading the shoulders of a high-pitching horse so that one might see the tense muscles.

"What's the matter? You and the Little Doctor have a falling out?"

"Not very bad," Chip's tone was open to several interpretations. Cal interpreted it as a denial.

"Sick?" He asked next.

"Yes!" said Chip, shortly and falsely.

"We'll call the doctor in, then," volunteered Jack Bates.

"I don't think you will. When I'm sick enough for that I'll let you know. I'm going to bed."

"Aw, come on and let him alone. Chip's able t' take care of himself, I guess," said Weary, mercifully, holding open the door.

They trooped out, and the last heard of them was Cal, remarking:

"Gee whiz! I'd have t' be ready t' croak before I'd miss this chance uh dealing old Dunk misery."

Chip sat where they had left him, staring unseeingly down at the uncompleted sketch. His cigarette went out, but he did not roll a fresh one and held the half-burned stub abstractedly between his lips, set in bitter lines.

Why should he care what a slip of a girl thought

of him? He didn't care; he only—that thought he did not follow to the end, but started immediately on a new one. He supposed he was ignorant, according to Eastern standards. Lined up alongside Dr. Cecil Granthum—damn him!—he would cut a sorry figure, no doubt. He had never seen the outside of a college, let alone imbibing learning within one. He had learned some of the wisdom which nature teaches those who can read her language, and he had read much, lying on his stomach under a summer sky, while the cattle grazed all around him and his horse cropped the sweet grasses within reach of his hand. He could repeat whole pages of Shakespeare, and of Scott, and Bobbie Burns—he'd like to try Dr. Cecil on some of them and see who came out ahead. Still, he was ignorant—and none realized it more keenly and bitterly than did Chip.

He rested his chin in his hand and brooded over his comfortless past and cheerless future. He could just remember his mother—and he preferred not to remember his father, who was less kind to him than were strangers. That was his past. And the future—always to be a cow-puncher? There was his knack for drawing; if he could study and practice, perhaps even the Little Doctor would not dare call him ignorant then. Not that he cared for what she might say or might not say, but a fellow can't help hating to be reminded of something that he knows better than anyone else—and that is not pleasant, however you may try to cover up the unsightliness of it.

If Dr. Cecil Granthum—damn him!—had been kicked into the world and made to fight fate with tender, childish little fists but lately outgrown their baby dimples, as had been *his* lot, would he have amounted to anything, either? Maybe Dr. Cecil would have grown up just common and ignorant and fit for nothing better than to furnish amusement to girl doctors with dimples and big, gray eyes and a way of laughing. He'd like to show that little woman that she didn't know all about him yet. It wasn't too late—he was only twenty-four—he would study, and work, and climb to where she must look up, not down, to him—if she cared enough to look at all. It wasn't too late. He would quit gambling and save his money, and by next winter he'd have enough to go somewhere and learn to make pictures that amounted to something. He'd show her!

After reiterating this resolve in several emphatic forms, Chip's spirits grew perceptibly lighter—so much so that he rolled a fresh cigarette and finished the drawing in his hands, which demonstrated the manner in which a particularly snaky broncho had taken a fall out of Jack Bates in the corral that morning.

Next day, early in the afternoon, the round-up climbed the grade and started on its long trip over the range, and, after they had gone, the ranch seemed very quiet and very lonely to the Little Doctor, who revenged herself by snubbing Dunk so unmercifully that he announced his intention of taking the next train for Butte, where he lived in the luxury of rich bachelorhood. As the Little Doctor showed no symptoms of repenting, he rode sullenly away to Dry Lake, and she employed the rest of the afternoon writing a full and decidedly prejudiced account to Dr. Cecil of her quarrel with Chip, whom, she said, she quite hated.

CHAPTER X.

What Whizzer Did.

"I guess Happy lost some of his horses, las' night," said Slim at the breakfast table next morning. Slim had been kept at the ranch to look after the fences and the ditches, and was doing full justice to the expert cookery of the Countess.

"What makes yuh think that?" The Old Man poised a bit of tender, broiled steak upon the end of his fork.

"They's a bunch hangin' around the upper fence, an' Whizzer's among 'em. I'd know that long-legged snake ten miles away."

The Little Doctor looked up quickly. She had never before heard of a "long-legged snake"—but then, she had not yet made the acquaintance of Whizzer.

"Well, maybe you better run 'em into the corral

and hold 'em till Shorty sends some one after 'em," suggested the Old Man.

"I never c'd run 'em in alone, not with Whizzer in the bunch," objected Slim. "He's the orneriest cayuse in Chouteau County."

"Whizzer'll make a rattlin' good saddle horse some day, when he's broke gentle," argued the Old Man.

"Huh! I don't envy Chip the job uh breakin' him, though," grunted Slim, as he went out of the door.

After breakfast the Little Doctor visited Silver and fed him his customary ration of lump sugar, helped the Countess tidy the house, and then found herself at a loss for something to do. She stood looking out into the hazy sunlight which lay warm on hill and coulee.

"I think I'll go up above the grade and make a sketch of the ranch," she said to the Countess, and hastily collected her materials.

Down by the creek a "cotton-tail" sprang out of her way and kicked itself out of sight beneath a bowlder. The Little Doctor stood and watched till he disappeared, before going on again. Further up the bluff a striped snake gave her a shivery surprise before he glided sinuously away under a sagebush. She crossed the grade and climbed the steep bluff beyond, searching for a comfortable place to work.

A little higher, she took possession of a great, gray bowlder jutting like a giant table from the gravelly soil. She walked out upon it and looked down—a sheer drop of ten or twelve feet to the barren, yellow slope below.

"I suppose it is perfectly solid," she soliloquized and stamped one stout, little boot, to see if the rock would tremble. If human emotions are possible to a heart of stone, the rock must have been greatly amused at the test. It stood firm as the hills around it.

Della sat down and looked below at the house—a doll's house; at the toy corrals and tiny sheds and stables. Slim, walking down the hill, was a mere pigmy—a short, waddling insect. At least, to a girl unused to gazing from a height, each object seemed absurdly small. Flying U coulee stretched away to the west, with a silver ribbon drawn carelessly through it with many a twist and loop, fringed with a tender green of young leaves. Away and beyond stood the Bear Paws, hazily blue, with splotches of purple shadows.

"I don't blame J. G. for loving this place," thought the Little Doctor, drinking in the intoxication of the West with every breath she drew.

She had just become absorbed in her work when a clatter arose from the grade below, and a dozen horses, headed by a tall, rangy sorrel she surmised was Whizzer, dashed down the hill. Weary and Chip galloped close behind. They did not look up, and so passed without seeing her. They were talking and laughing in very good spirits—which the Little Doctor resented, for some inexplicable reason. She heard them call to Slim to open the corral gate, and saw Slim run to do their bidding. She forgot her sketching and watched Whizzer dodge and bolt back, and Chip tear through the creek bed after him at peril of life and limb.

Back and forth, round and round went Whizzer, running almost through the corral gate, then swerving suddenly and evading his pursuers with an ease which bordered closely on the marvelous. Slim saddled a horse and joined in the chase, and the Old Man climbed upon the fence and shouted advice which no one heard and would not have heeded if they had.

As the chase grew in earnestness and excitement, the sympathies of the Little Doctor were given unreservedly to Whizzer. Whenever a particularly clever maneuver of his set the men to swearing, she clapped her hands in sincere, though unheard and unappreciated, applause.

"Good boy!" she cried, approvingly, when he dodged Chip and whirled through the big gate which the Old Man had unwittingly left open. J. G. leaned perilously forward and shook his fist unavailingly. Whizzer tossed head and heels alternately and scurried up the path to the very door of the kitchen, where he swung round and looked back down the hill snorting triumph.

"Shoo, there!" shrilled the Countess, shaking her dish towel at him.

"Who-oo-oof-f," snorted he disdainfully and trotted leisurely round the corner.

Chip galloped up the hill, his horse running heavily. After him came Weary, liberally applying quirt and mild invective. At the house they parted and headed the fugitive toward the stables. He shot through the big gate, lifting his heels viciously at the Old Man as he passed, whirled around the stable and trotted haughtily past Slim into the corral of his own accord, quite as if he had meant to do so all along.

"Did you ever!" exclaimed the Little Doctor, disgustedly, from her perch. "Whizzer, I'm ashamed of you! *I* wouldn't have given in like that—but you gave them a chase, didn't you, my beauty?"

The boys flung themselves off their tired horses and went up to the house to beg the Countess for a lunch, and Della turned resolutely to her sketching again.

She was just beginning to forget that the world

held aught but soft shadows, mellow glow and hazy perspective, when a subdued uproar reached her from below. She drew an uncertain line or two, frowned and laid her pencil resignedly in her lap.

"It's of no use. I can't do a thing till those cow-punchers take themselves and their bronchos off the ranch—and may it be soon!" she told herself, disconsolately and not oversincerely. The best of us are not above trying to pull the wool over our own eyes, at times.

In reality their brief presence made the near future seem very flat and insipid to the Little Doctor. It was washing all the color out of the picture, and leaving it a dirty gray. She gazed moodily down at the whirl of dust in the corral, where Whizzer was struggling to free himself from the loop Chip had thrown with his accustomed, calm precision. Whatever Chip did he did thoroughly, with no slurring of detail. Whizzer was fain to own himself fairly caught.

"Oh, he's got you fast, my beauty!" sighed the Little Doctor, woefully. "Why didn't you jump over the fence—I think you *could*—and run, run, to freedom?" She grew quite melodramatic over the humiliation of the horse she had chosen to champion, and glared resentfully when Chip threw his saddle, with no gentle hand, upon the sleek back and tightened the cinches with a few strong, relentless yanks.

"Chip, you're an ugly, mean-tempered—that's right, Whizzer! Kick him if you can—I'll stand by you!" This assertion, you understand, was purely figurative; the Little Doctor would have hesitated long before attempting to carry it out literally.

"Now, Whizzer, when he tries to ride you, don't you let him! Throw him clear—over—the *stable*—so there!"

Perhaps Whizzer understood the command in some mysterious, telepathic manner. At any rate, he set himself straightway to obey it, and there was not a shadow of doubt but that he did his best—but Chip did not choose to go over the stable. Instead of doing so, he remained in the saddle and changed ends with his quirt, to the intense rage of the Little Doctor, who nearly cried.

"Oh, you brute! You fiend! I'll never speak to you again as long as I live! Oh, Whizzer, you poor fellow, why do you let him abuse you so? Why *don't* you throw him clean off the ranch?"

This is exactly what Whizzer was trying his best to do, and Whizzer's best was exceedingly bad for his rider, as a general thing. But Chip calmly refused to be thrown, and Whizzer, who was no fool, suddenly changed his tactics and became so meek that his champion on the bluff felt tempted to despise him for such servile submission to a tyrant in brown chaps and gray hat—I am transcribing the facts according to the Little Doctor's interpretation.

She watched gloomily while Whizzer, in whose brain lurked no thought of submission, galloped steadily along behind the bunch which Slim made haste to liberate, and bided his time. She had expected better—rather, worse—of him than that. She had not dreamed he would surrender so tamely. As they crossed the Hog's Back and climbed the steep grade just below her, she eyed him reproachfully and said again:

"Whizzer, I'm ashamed of you!"

It did certainly seem that Whizzer heard and felt the pricking of pride at the reproof. He made a feint at being frightened by a jack rabbit which sprang out from the shade of a rock and bounced down the hill like a rubber ball. As if Whizzer had never seen a jack rabbit before!—he who had been born and reared upon the range among them! It was a feeble excuse at the best, but he made the most of it and lost no time seeking a better.

He stopped short, sidled against Weary's horse and snorted. Chip, in none the best humor with him, jerked the reins savagely and dug him with his spurs, and Whizzer, resenting the affront, whirled and bounded high in the air. Back down the grade he bucked with the high, rocking, crooked jumps which none but a Western cayuse can make, while Weary turned in his saddle and watched with sharp-drawn breaths. There was nothing else that he could do.

Chip was by no means passive. For every jump that Whizzer made, the rawhide quirt landed across his flaring nostrils, and the locked rowels of Chip's spurs raked the sorrel sides from cinch to flank, leaving crimson streams behind them.

Wild with rage at this clinging cow-puncher whom he could not dislodge, who stung his sides and head like the hornets in the meadow, Whizzer gathered himself for a mighty leap as he reached the Hog's Back. Like a wire spring released, he shot into the air, shook himself in one last, desperate hope of victory, and, failing, came down with not a joint in his legs and turned a somersault.

A moment, and he struggled to his feet and limped painfully away, crushed and beaten in spirit.

Chip did not struggle. He lay, a long length of brown chaps, pink-and-white shirt and gray hat, just where he had fallen.

The Little Doctor never could remember getting down that bluff, and her sketching materials went to amuse the jack rabbits and the birds. Fast as she flew, Weary was before her and had raised Chip's head upon one arm. She knelt beside him in the dust, hovering over the white face and still form like a pitying, little gray angel. Weary looked at her impersonally, but neither of them spoke in those first, breathless moments.

The Old Man, who had witnessed the accident, came puffing laboriously up the hill, taking the short cut straight across from the stable.

"Is he—*dead?*" he yelled while he scrambled.

Weary turned his head long enough to look down at him, with the same impersonal gaze he had bestowed upon the Little Doctor, but he did not answer the question. He could not, for he did not know. The Little Doctor seemed not to have heard.

The Old Man redoubled his exertions and reached them very much out of breath.

"Is he dead, Dell?" he repeated in an awestruck tone. He feared she would say yes.

The Little Doctor had taken possession of the brown head. She looked up at her brother, a very unprofessional pallor upon her face, and down at the long, brown lashes and at the curved, sensitive lips which held no hint of red. She pressed the face closer to her breast and shook her head. She could not speak, just then, for the griping ache that was in her throat.

"One of the best men on the ranch gone under, just when we need help the worst!" complained the Old Man. "Is he hurt bad?"

"J. G.," began the Little Doctor in a voice all the fiercer for being suppressed, "I want you to kill that horse. Do you hear? If you don't do it, I will!"

"You won't have to, if old Splinter goes down and out," said Weary, with quiet meaning, and the Little Doctor gave him a grateful flash of gray eyes.

"How bad is he hurt?" repeated the Old Man, impatiently. "You're supposed t' be a doctor—don't you know?"

"He has a scalp wound which does not seem serious," said she in an attempt to be matter-of-fact, "and his left collar bone is broken."

"Doggone it! A broken collar bone ain't mended overnight."

"No," acquiesced the Little Doctor, "it isn't."

These last two remarks Chip heard. He opened his eyes and looked straight up into the gray ones above—a long, questioning, rebellious look. He tried then to rise, to free himself from the bitter ecstasy of those soft, enfolding arms. Only a broken collar bone! Good thing it was no worse! Ugh! A spasm of pain contracted his features and drew beads of moisture to his forehead. The spurned arms once more felt the dead weight of him.

"What is it?" The Little Doctor's voice called to him from afar.

Must he answer? He wanted to drift on and on——

"Can you tell me where the pain is?"

Pain? Oh, yes, there had been pain—but he wanted to drift. He opened his eyes again reluctantly; again the pain clutched him.

"It's—my—foot."

For the first time the eyes of the Little Doctor left his face and traveled downward to the spurred boots. One was twisted in a horrible unnatural position that told the agonizing truth—a badly dislocated ankle. They returned quickly to the face, and swam full of blinding tears—such as a doctor should not succumb to. He was not drifting into oblivion now; his teeth were not digging into his lower lip for nothing, she knew.

"Weary," she said, forgetting to call him properly by name, "ride to the house and get my medicine case—the little black one. The Countess knows—and have Slim bring something to carry him home on. And—*ride!*"

Weary was gone before she had finished, and he certainly "rode."

"You'll have another crippled cow-puncher on yer hands, first thing yuh know," grumbled the Old Man, anxiously, as he watched Weary race recklessly down the hill.

The Little Doctor did not answer. She scarcely heard him. She was stroking the hair back from Chip's forehead softly, unconsciously, wondering why she had never before noticed the wave in it—but then, she had scarcely seen him with his hat off. How silky and soft it felt! And she had called him all sorts of mean names, and had wanted Whizzer to—she shuddered and turned sick at the memory of the thud when they struck the hard road together.

"Dell!" exclaimed the Old Man, "you're white's a rag. Doggone it, don't throw up yer hands at yer first case—brace up!"

Chip looked up at her curiously, forgetting the pain long enough to wonder at her whiteness. Did she have a heart, then, or was it a feminine trait to turn pale in every emergency? She had not turned so very white when those kids—he felt inclined to laugh, only for that cussed foot. Instead he relaxed his vigilance and a groan slipped out before he knew.

"Just a minute more and I'll ease the pain for you," murmured the girl, compassionately.

"All right—so long as you—don't—use—the stomach pump," he retorted, with a miserable makeshift of a laugh.

"What's that?" asked the Old Man, but no one explained.

The Little Doctor was struggling with the lump in her throat that he should try to joke about it.

Then Weary was back and holding the little, black case out to her. She seized it eagerly, slipping Chip's head to her knees that she might use her hands freely. There was no halting over the tiny vials, for she had decided just what she must do.

She laid something against Chip's closed lips.

"Swallow these," she said, and he obeyed her. "Weary—oh, you knew what to do, I see. There, lay the coat down there for a pillow."

Relieved of her burden, she rose and went to the poor, twisted foot.

Weary and the Old Man watched her go to work systematically and disclose the swollen, purpling ankle. Very gently she did it, and when she had administered a merciful anæsthetic, the enthusiasm of the Old Man demanded speech.

"Well, I'll be eternally doggoned! You're onto your job, Dell, doggoned if yuh ain't. I won't ever josh yuh again about yer doctorin'!"

"I wish you'd been around the time I smashed *my* ankle," commented Weary, fishing for his cigarette book; he was beginning to feel the need of a quieting smoke. “They hauled me forty miles, to Benton.”

“That must have been torture!” shuddered the Little Doctor. “A dislocated ankle is a most agonizing thing.”

“Yes,” assented Weary, striking a match, “it sure is, all right.”

CHAPTER XI.

Good Intentions.

"Mr. Davidson, have you nerve enough to help me replace this ankle? The Countess is too nervous, and J. G. is too awkward."

Chip was lying oblivious to his surroundings or his hurt in the sunny, south room which Dunk Whitaker chose to call his.

"I've never been accused of wanting nerve," grinned Weary. "I guess I can stand it if you can." And a very efficient assistant he proved himself to be.

When the question of a nurse arose, when all had been done that could be done and Weary had gone, the Little Doctor found herself involved in an argument with the Countess. The Countess wanted them to send for Bill. Bill jűst thought the world and all of Chip, she declared, and would just love to come. She was positive that Bill was the very one they needed, and the Little Doctor, who had conceived a violent dislike for Bill, a smirky, self-satisfied youth addicted to chewing tobacco, red neckties and a perennial grin, was equally positive he was the very one they did *not* want. In despair she retrenched herself behind the assertion that Chip should choose for himself.

"I just know he'll choose Bill," crowed the Countess after the flicker of the doctor's skirts.

Chip turned his head rebelliously upon the pillow and looked up at her. Something in his eyes brought to mind certain stormy crises in the headstrong childhood of the Little Doctor—crises in which she was forced to submission very much against her will. It was the same mutinous surrender to overwhelming strength, the same futile defiance of fate.

"I came to ask you who you would rather have to nurse you," she said, trying to keep the erratic color from crimsoning her cheeks. You see, she had never had a patient of her very own before, and there were certain embarrassing complications in having this particular young man in charge.

Chip's eyes wandered wistfully to the window,

where a warm, spring breeze flapped the curtains in and out.

"How long have I got to lie here?" he asked, reluctantly.

"A month, at the least—more likely six weeks," she said with kind bluntness. It was best he should know the worst at once.

Chip turned his face bitterly to the wall for a minute and traced an impossible vine to its breaking point where the paper had not been properly matched. Twenty miles away the boys were hurrying through their early dinner that they might catch up their horses for the afternoon's work. And they had two good feet to walk on, two sound arms to subdue restless horseflesh and he was not there! He could fairly smell the sweet, trampled sod as the horses circled endlessly inside the rope corral, and hear them snort when a noose swished close. He wondered who would get his string to ride, and what they would do with his bed.

He didn't need it, now; he would lie on wire

springs, instead of on the crisp, prairie grass. He would be waited on like a yearling baby and——

"The Countess just knows you will choose Bill," interrupted a whimsical girl voice.

Chip said something which the Little Doctor did not try to hear distinctly. "Don't she think I've had enough misery dealt me for once?" he asked, without taking his eyes from the poor, broken vine. He rather pitied the vine—it seemed to have been badly used by fate, just as he had been. He was sure it had not wanted to stop right there on that line, as it had been forced to do. *He* had not wanted to stop, either. He——

"She says Bill would just love to come," said the voice, with a bit of a laugh in it.

Chip, turning his head back suddenly, looked into the gray eyes and felt inexplicably cheered. He almost believed she understood something of what it all meant to him. And she mercifully refrained from spoken pity, which he felt he could not have borne just then. His lips took back some of their curve.

"You tell her I wouldn't just love to have him," he said, grimly.

"I'd never dare. She dotes on Bill. Whom *do* you want?"

"When it comes to that, I don't want anybody. But if you could get Johnny Beckman to come——"

"Oh, I will—I'll go myself, to make sure of him. Which one is Johnny?"

"Johnny's the red-headed one," said Chip.

"But—they're *all*——"

"Yes, but his head is several shades redder than any of the others," interrupted he, quite cheerfully.

The Little Doctor, observing the twinkle in his eyes, felt her spirits rise wonderfully. She could not bear that hurt, rebellious, lonely look which they had worn.

"I'll bring him—but I may have to chloroform the Countess to get him into the house. You must try to sleep, while I'm gone—and don't fret—will you? You'll get well all the quicker for taking things easily."

Chip smiled faintly at this wholesome advice, and

the Little Doctor laid her hand shyly upon his forehead to test its temperature, drew down the shade over the south window, and left him in dim, shadowy coolness to sleep.

She came again before she started for Johnny, and found him wide awake and staring hungrily at the patch of blue sky visible through the window which faced the East.

"You'll have to learn to obey orders better than this," she said, severely, and took quiet possession of his wrist. "I told you not to fret about being hurt. I know you hate it——"

Chip flushed a little under her touch and the tone in which she spoke the last words. It seemed to mean that she hated it even more than he did, having him helpless in the house with her. It hadn't been so long since she had told him plainly how little she liked him. He was not going to forget, in a hurry!

"Why don't you send me to the hospital?" he demanded, brusquely. "I could stand the trip, all right."

The Little Doctor, the color coming and going in her cheeks, pressed her cool fingers against his forehead.

"Because I want you here to practice on. Do you think I'd let such a chance escape?"

After she was gone, Chip found some things to puzzle over. He felt that he was no match for the Little Doctor, and for the first time in his life he deeply regretted his ignorance of woman nature.

When the dishes were done, the Countess put her resentment behind her and went in to sit with Chip, with the best of intentions. The most disagreeable trait of some disagreeable people is that their intentions are invariably good. She had her "crochy work," and Chip groaned inwardly when he saw her settle herself comfortably in a rocking-chair and unwind her thread. The Countess had worked hard all her life, and her hands were red and big-jointed. There was no pleasure in watching their clever manipulation of the little, steel hook. If it had been the Little Doctor's hands, now—Chip turned again to the decapitated, pale blue vine with its pink flowers and no leaves. The Countess counted off "chain 'leven" and began in a constrained tone, such as some well-meaning people employ against helpless sick folk.

"How're yuh feelin' now? Yuh want a drink, or anything?"

Chip did not want a drink, and he felt all right, he guessed.

The Countess thought to cheer him a little.

"Well, I do think it's too bad yuh got t' lay here all through this purty spring weather. If it had been in the winter, when it's cold and stormy outside, a person wouldn't mind it s' much. I know yuh must feel purty blew over it, fer yuh was always sech a hand t' be tearin' around the country on the dead run, seems like. I always told Mary 't you'n Weary always rode like the sheriff wa'nt more'n a mile b'hind yuh. An' I s'pose you feel it all the more, seein' the round-up's jest startin' out. Weary said yuh was playin' big luck, if yuh only knew enough t' cash in yer chips at the right time, but he's afraid yuh wouldn't be watching the game close enough an' ud lose yer pile. I don't know what he was drivin' at, an' I guess he didn't neither. It's too bad, anyway. I guess yuh didn't expect t' wind up in bed when yuh rode off up the hill. But as the sayin' is: 'Man plans an' God displans,' an' I guess it's so. Here yuh are, laid up fer the summer, Dell says—the las' thing on earth, I guess, that yuh was lookin' fer. An' yuh rode buckin' bronks right along, too. I never looked fer Whizzer t' buck yuh off, I must say—yuh got the name uh bein' sech a good rider, too. But they say 't the pitcher 't's always goin' t' the well is bound t' git busted sometime, an' I guess your turn come t' git busted. Anyway——"

"I didn't get bucked off," broke in Chip, angrily. A "bronch fighter" is not more jealous of his sweetheart than of his reputation as a rider. "A fellow can't very well make a pretty ride while his horse is turning a somersault."

"Oh, well, I didn't happen t' se it—I thought Weary said 't yuh got throwed off on the Hog's

Back. Anyway, I don't know's it makes much difference how yuh happened t' hit the ground——"

"I guess it does make a difference," cried Chip, hotly. His eyes took on the glitter of fever. "It makes a whole heap of difference, let me tell you! I'd like to hear Weary or anybody else stand up and tell me that I got bucked off. I may be pretty badly smashed up, but I'd come pretty near showing him where he stood."

"Oh, well, yuh needn't go t' work an' git mad about it," remonstrated the Countess, dropping her thread in her perturbation at his excitement. The spool rolled under the bed and she was obliged to get down upon her knees and claw it back, and she jarred the bed and set Chip's foot to hurting again something awful.

When she finally secured the spool and resumed her chair, Chip's eyes were tightly closed, but the look of his mouth and the flush in his cheeks, together with his quick breathing, precluded the belief that he was asleep. The Countess was not a fool—she saw at once that fever, which the Little Doctor had feared, was fast taking hold of him. She rolled her half yard of "edging" around the spool of thread, jabbed the hook through the lump and went out and told the Old Man that Chip was getting worse every minute—which was the truth.

The Old Man knocked the ashes out of his pipe and went in to look at him.

"Did Weary say I got bucked off?" demanded the sick man before the Old Man was fairly in the room. "If he did, he lied, that's all. I didn't think Weary'd do me dirt like that—I thought he'd stand by me if anybody would. He knows I wasn't throwed. I——"

"Here, young fellow," put in the Old Man, calmly, "don't yuh git t' rampagin' around over nothin'! You turn over there an' go t' sleep."

"I'll be hanged if I will!" retorted Chip. "If Weary's taken to lying about me I'll have it out with him if I break all the rest of my bones doing it. Do you think I'm going to stand a thing like that? I'll see——"

"Easy there, doggone it. I never heard Weary

say't yuh got bucked off. Whizzer turned over on his head, 's near as I c'd make out fer dust. I took it he turned a summerset."

Chip's befogged brain caught at the last word.

"Yes, that's just what he did. It beats me how Weary could say, or even think, that I—it was the jack rabbit first—and I told her the supply was limited—and if we do furnish lots of amusement—but I guess I made her understand I wasn't so easy as she took me to be. She——"

"Hey?" The Old Man could hardly be blamed for losing the drift of Chip's rapid utterances.

"If we want to get them rounded up before the dance, I'll—it's a good thing it wasn't poison, for seven dead kids at once——"

The Old Man knew something about sickness himself. He hurried out, returning in a moment with a bowl of cool water and a fringed napkin which he pilfered from the dining-room table, wisely intending to bathe Chip's head.

But Chip would have none of him or his wise intentions. He jerked the wet napkin from the Old

Man's fingers and threw it down behind the bed, knocked up the bowl of water into the Old Man's face and called him some very bad names. The Countess came and looked in, and Chip hurled a pillow at her and called her a bad name also, so that she retreated to the kitchen with her feelings very much hurt. After that Chip had the south room to himself until the Little Doctor returned with Johnny.

The Old Man, looking rather scared, met her on the porch. The Little Doctor read his face before she was off her horse.

"What's the matter? Is he worse?" she demanded, abruptly.

"That's fer you t' find out. *I* ain't no doctor. He got on the fight, a while back, an' took t' throwin' things an' usin' langwidge. He can't git out uh bed, thank the Lord, or we'd be takin' t' the hills by now."

"Then somebody has it to answer for. He was all right when I left him, two hours ago, with not a sign of fever. Has the Countess been pestering him?"

"No," said the Countess, popping her head out of the kitchen window and speaking in an aggrieved tone, "I hope I never pester anybody. I went an' done all I could t' cheer 'im up, an' that's all the thanks I git fer it. I must say some folks ain't overburdened with gratitude, anyhow."

The Little Doctor did not wait to hear her out. She went straight to the south room, pulling off her gloves on the way. The pillow on the floor told her an eloquent tale, and she sighed as she picked it up and patted some shape back into it. Chip stared at her with wide, bright eyes from the bed.

"I don't suppose Dr. Cecil Granthum would throw pillows at anybody!" he remarked, sarcastically, as she placed it very gently under his head.

"Perhaps, if the provocation was great enough. What have they been doing to you?"

"Did Weary say I got bucked off?" he demanded, excitedly.

The Little Doctor was counting his pulse, and waited till she had finished. It was a high number—much higher than she liked.

"No, Weary didn't. How could he? You didn't, you know. I saw it all from the bluff, and I know the horse turned over upon you. It's a wonder you weren't killed outright. Now, don't worry about it any more—I expect it was the Countess told you that. Weary hated dreadfully to leave you. I wonder if you know how much he thinks of you? I didn't, till I saw how he looked when you—here, drink this, all of it. You've got to sleep, you see."

There was a week when the house was kept very still, and the south room very cool and shadowy, and Chip did not much care who it was that ministered to him—only that the hands of the Little Doctor were always soft and soothing on his head and he wished she would keep them there always, when he was himself enough to wish anything coherently.

CHAPTER XII.

"The Last Stand."

To use a trite expression and say that Chip "fought his way back to health" would be simply stating a fact and stating it mildly. He went about it much as he would go about gentling a refractory broncho, and with nearly the same results.

His ankle, however, simply could not be hurried or bluffed into premature soundness, and the Little Doctor was at her wits' end to keep Chip from fretting himself back into fever, once he was safely pulled out of it. She made haste to explain the bit of overheard conversation, which he harped on more than he dreamed, when his head went light in that first week, and so established a more friendly feeling between them.

Still, there was a certain aloofness about him which she could not conquer, try as she might. Just so far they were comrades—beyond, Chip walked moodily alone. The Little Doctor did not like that overmuch. She preferred to know that she fairly understood her friends and was admitted, sometimes, to their full confidence. She did not relish bumping her head against a blank wall that was too high to look over or to climb, and in which there seemed to be no door.

To be sure, he talked freely, and amusingly, of his adventures and of the places he had known, but it was always an impersonal recital, and told little of his real self or his real feelings. Still, when she asked him, he told her exactly what he thought about things, whether his opinion pleased her or not.

There were times when he would sit in the old Morris chair and smoke and watch her make lacey stuff in a little, round frame. Battenberg, she said it was. He loved to see her fingers manipulate the needle and the thread, and take wonderful pains with her work—but once she showed him a butterfly whose wings did not quite match, and he pointed it out to her. She had been listening to him tell a story of Indians and cowboys and with some wild riding mixed into it, and—well, she used the wrong stitch, but no one would notice it in a thousand years. This, her argument.

"You'll always know the mistake's there, and you won't get the satisfaction out of it you would if it was perfect, would you?" argued Chip, letting his eyes dwell on her face more than was good for him.

The Little Doctor pouted her lips in a way to tempt a man all he could stand, and snipped out the wing with her scissors and did it over.

So with her painting. She started a scene in the edge of the Bad Lands down the river. Chip knew the place well. There was a heated discussion over the foreground, for the Little Doctor wanted him to sketch in some Indian tepees and some squaws for her, and Chip absolutely refused to do so. He said there were no Indians in that country, and it would spoil the whole picture, anyway. The Little Doctor threatened to sketch them herself, drawing on her imagination and what little she knew of Indians, but something in his eyes stayed her hand. She left the easel in disgust and refused to touch it again for a week.

She was to spend a long day with Miss Satterly, the schoolma'am, and started off soon after breakfast one morning.

"I hope you'll find something to keep you out of mischief while I'm gone," she remarked, with a pretty, authoritative air. "Make him take his medicine, Johnny, and don't let him have the crutches. Well, I think I shall hide them to make sure."

"I wish to goodness you had that picture done," grumbled Chip. "It seems to me you're doing a heap of running around, lately. Why don't you finish it up? Those lonesome hills are getting on my nerves."

"I'll cover it up," said she.

"Let it be. I like to look at them." Chip leaned back in his chair and watched her, a hunger greater than he knew in his eyes. It was most awfully lonesome when she was gone all day, and last night she had been writing all the evening to Dr. Cecil Granthum—damn him! Chip always hitched that invective to the unknown doctor's name, for some reason he saw fit not to explain to himself. He didn't see what she could find to write about so much, for his part. And he did hate a long day with no one but Johnny to talk to.

He craned his neck to keep her in view as long as possible, drew a long, discontented breath and settled himself more comfortably in the chair where he spent the greater part of his waking hours.

"Hand me the tobacco, will you, kid?"

He fished his cigarette book from his pocket. "Thanks!" He tore a narrow strip from the paper and sifted in a little tobacco.

"Now a match, kid, and then you're done."

Johnny placed the matches within easy reach, shoved a few magazines close to Chip's elbow, and stretched himself upon the floor with a book.

Chip lay back against the cushions and smoked lazily, his eyes half closed, dreaming rather than thinking. The unfinished painting stood facing him upon its easel, and his eyes idly fixed upon it. He knew the place so well. Jagged pinnacles, dotted here and there with scrubby pines, hemmed in a tiny basin below—where was blank canvas. He went mentally over the argument again, and from that drifted to a scene he had witnessed in that same basin, one day—but that was in the winter. Dirty gray snow drifts, where a chinook had cut them, and icy side hills made the place still drearier. And the foreground—if the Little Doctor could get *that,* now, she would be doing something!—ah! that foreground. A poor, half-starved range cow with her calf which the round-up had overlooked in the fall, stood at bay against a steep cut bank. Before them squatted five great, gaunt wolves intent upon fresh beef for their supper. But the cow's horns were long, and sharp, and threatening, and the calf snuggled close to her side, shivering with the cold and the fear of death. The wolves licked their cruel lips and their eyes gleamed hungrily—but the eyes of the cow answered them, gleam for gleam. If it could be put upon canvas just as he had seen it, with the bitter, biting cold of a frozen chinook showing gray and sinister in the slaty sky——

"Kid!"

"Huh?" Johnny struggled reluctantly back to Montana.

"Get me the Little Doctor's paint and truck, over on that table, and slide that easel up here."

Johnny stared, opened his mouth to speak, then wisely closed it and did as he was bidden. Philosophically he told himself it was Chip's funeral, if the Little Doctor made a kick.

"All right, kid." Chip tossed the cigarette stub out of the window. "You can go ahead and read, now. Lock the door first, and don't you bother me—not on your life."

Then Chip plunged headlong into the Bad Lands, so to speak.

A few dabs of dirty white, here and there, a wholly original manipulation of the sky—what mattered the method, so he attained the result? Half an hour, and the hills were clutched in the chill embrace of a "frozen chinook" such as the Little Doctor had never seen in her life. But Johnny, peeping surreptitiously over Chip's shoulder, stared at the change; then, feeling the spirit of it, shivered in sympathy with the barren hills.

"Hully gee," he muttered under his breath, "he's sure a corker t' paint cold that fair makes yer nose sting." And he curled up in a chair behind, where he could steal a look, now and then, without fear of detection.

But Chip was dead to all save that tiny basin in the Bad Lands—to the wolves and their quarry. His eyes burned as they did when the fever held him; each cheek bone glowed flaming red.

As wolf after wolf appeared with what, to Johnny, seemed uncanny swiftness, and squatted, grinning and sinister, in a relentless half circle, the book slipped unheeded to the floor with a clatter that failed to rouse the painter, whose ears were dulled to all else than the pitiful blat of a shivering, panic-stricken calf whose nose sought his mother's side for her comforting warmth and protection.

The Countess rapped on the door for dinner, and Johnny rose softly and tiptoed out to quiet her. May he be forgiven the lies he told that day, of

"THE LAST STAND." Page 177.

how Chip's head ached and he wanted to sleep and must not be disturbed, by strict orders of the Little Doctor. The Countess, to whom the very name of the Little Doctor was a fetich, closed all intervening doors and walked on her toes in the kitchen, and Johnny rejoiced at the funeral quiet which rested upon the house.

Faster flew the brush. Now the eyes of the cow glared desperate defiance. One might almost see her bony side, ruffled by the cutting north wind, heave with her breathing. She was fighting death for herself and her baby—but for how long? Already the nose of one great, gray beast was straight uplifted, sniffing, impatient. Would they risk a charge upon those lowered horns? The dark pines shook their feathery heads hopelessly. A little while perhaps, and then——

Chip laid down the brush and sank back in the chair. Was the sun so low? He could do no more—yes, he took up a brush and added the title: "The Last Stand."

He was very white, and his hand shook. Johnny

leaned over the back of the chair, his eyes glued to the picture.

"Gee," he muttered, huskily, "I'd like t' git a whack at them wolves once."

Chip turned his head until he could look at the lad's face. "What do you think of it, kid?" he asked, shakily.

Johnny did not answer for a moment. It was hard to put what he felt into words. "I dunno just how t' say it," he said, gropingly, at last, "but it makes me want t' go gunnin' fer them wolves b'fore they hamstring her. It—well—it don't seem t' me like it was a pitcher, somehow. It seems like the reel thing, kinda."

Chip moved his head languidly upon the cushion.

"I'm dead tired, kid. No, I'm not hungry, nor I don't want any coffee, or anything. Just roll this chair over to the bed, will you? I'm—dead—tired."

Johnny was worried. He did not know what the Little Doctor would say, for Chip had not eaten his dinner, or taken his medicine. Somehow there had been that in his face that had made Johnny afraid to speak to him. He went back to the easel and looked long at the picture, his heart bursting with rage that he could not take his rifle and shoot those merciless, grinning brutes. Even after he had drawn the curtain before it and stood the easel in its accustomed place, he kept lifting the curtain to take another look at that wordless tragedy of the West.

CHAPTER XIII.

Art Critics.

It was late the next forenoon when the Little Doctor, feeling the spirit of artistic achievement within her, gathered up brushes and paints for a couple hours' work. Chip, sitting by the window smoking a cigarette, watched her uneasily from the tail of his eye. Looking back to yesterday's "spasm," as he dubbed it mentally, he was filled with a great and unaccountable shyness. What had seemed so real to him then he feared to-day to face, as trivial and weak.

He wanted to cry "Stop!" when she laid hand to the curtain, but he looked, instead, out across the coulee to the hills beyond, the blood surging unevenly through his veins. He felt when she drew the cloth aside; she stopped short off in the middle of telling him something Miss Satterly had said—some whimsical thing—and he could hear his heart pounding in the silence which followed. The little, nickel alarm clock tick-tick-ticked with such maddening precision and speed that Chip wanted to shy a book at it, but his eyes never left the rocky bluff opposite, and the clock ticked merrily on.

One minute—two—the silence was getting unbearable. He could not endure another second. He looked toward her; she stood, one hand full of brushes, gazing, white-faced, at "The Last Stand." As he looked, a tear rolled down the cheek nearest him and compelled him to speech.

"What's the matter?" His voice seemed to him rough and brutal, but he did not mean it so.

The Little Doctor drew a long, quivering breath. "Oh, the poor, brave thing!" she said, in a hushed tone. She turned sharply away and sat down.

"I expect I spoiled your picture, all right—but I told you I'd get into mischief if you went gadding around and left me alone."

The Little Doctor stealthily wiped her eyes, hoping to goodness Chip had not seen that they had need of wiping.

"Why didn't you tell me you could paint like that?" She turned upon him fiercely. "Here you've sat and looked on at me daubing things up—and if I'd known you could do better than——" Looking again at the canvas she forgot to finish. The fascination of it held her.

"I'm not in the habit of going around the country shouting what I don't know," said Chip, defensively. "You've taken heaps of lessons, and I never did. I just noticed the color of everything, and—oh, I don't know—it's in me to do those things. I can't help trying to paint and draw."

"I suppose old Von Heim would have something to say of your way of doing clouds—but you got the effect, though—better than he did, sometimes. And that cow—I can see her breathe, I tell you! And the wolves—oh, don't sit there and smoke your everlasting cigarettes and look so stoical over it! What are you made of, anyway? Can't you feel proud? Oh, don't you know what you've done? I—I'd like to shake you—so now!"

"Well, I don't much blame you. I knew I'd no

business to meddle. Maybe, if you'll touch it up a little——"

"I'll not touch a brush to *that*. I—I'm afraid I might kill the cow." She gave a little, hysterical laugh.

"Don't you think you're rather excitable—for a doctor?" scoffed Chip, and her chin went up for a minute.

"I'd like t' kill them wolves," said Johnny, coming in just then.

"Turn the thing around, kid, so I can see it," commanded Chip, suddenly. "I worked at it yesterday till the colors all ran together and I couldn't tell much about it."

Johnny turned the easel, and Chip, looking, fell silent. Had *his* hand guided the brush while that scene grew from blank canvas to palpitating reality? Verily, he had "builded better than he knew." Something in his throat gripped, achingly and dry.

"Did anybody see it yesterday?" asked the Little Doctor.

"No—not unless the kid——"

"I never said a word about it," denied Johnny, hastily and vehemently. "I lied like the dickens. I said you had headache an' was tryin' t' sleep it off. I kep' the Countess teeterin' around on her toes all afternoon." Johnny giggled at the memory of it.

"Well, I'm going to call them all in and see what they say," declared she, starting for the door.

"I don't *think* you will," began Chip, rebelliously, blushing over his achievement like a girl over her graduation essay. "I don't want to be——"

"Well, we needn't tell them you did it," suggested she.

"Oh, if you're willing to shoulder the blame," compromised Chip, much relieved. He hated to be fussed over.

The Little Doctor regarded him attentively a moment, smiled queerly to herself and stood back to get a better view of the painting.

"I'll shoulder the blame—and maybe claim the glory. It was mine in the first place, you know." She watched him from under her lashes.

"Yes. it's yours, all right," said Chip, readily, but

something went out of his face and lodged rather painfully in the deepest corner of his heart. He ignored it proudly and smiled back at her.

"Do such things really happen, out here?" she asked, hurriedly.

"I'd tell a man!" said Chip, his eyes returning to the picture. "I was riding through that country last winter, and I came upon that very cow, just as you see her there, in that same basin. That's how I came to paint it into your foreground; I got to thinking about it, and I couldn't help trying to put it on canvas. Only, I opened up on the wolves with my six-shooter, and I got two; that big fellow ready to howl, there, and that one next the cut-bank. The rest broke out down the coulee and made for the breaks, where I couldn't follow. They——"

"Say! . Old Dunk's comin'," announced Johnny, hurrying in. "Why don't yuh let 'im see the pitcher an' think all the time the Little Doctor done it? Gee, it'd be great t' hear 'im go on an' praise it up, like he always does, an' not know the diffrunce."

"Johnny, you're a genius," cried she, effusively.

"Don't tell a soul that Chip had a brush in his hand yesterday, will you? He—he'd rather not have anyone know he did anything to the painting, you see."

"Aw, I won't tell," interrupted Johnny, gruffly, eying his divinity with distrust for the first time in his short acquaintance with her. Was she mean enough to claim it really? Just at first, as a joke, it would be fun, but afterward, oh, she wouldn't do a thing like that!

"Don't you bring Dunk in here," warned Chip, "or things might happen. I don't want to run up against him again till I've got two good feet to stand on."

Their relation was a thing to be watched over tenderly, since Chip's month of invalidism. Dunk had notions concerning master and servant, and concerning Chip as an individual. He did not fancy occupying the back bedroom while Chip reigned in his sunny south room, waited on, petted (Dunk applied the term petted) and amused indefatigably by the Little Doctor. And there had been a scene, short but exceeding "strenuous," over a pencil sketch which graphically portrayed an incident Dunk fain would forget—the incident of himself as a would-be broncho fighter, with Banjo, of vigilante fame, as the means of his downfall—physical, mental and spiritual. Dunk might, in time, have forgiven the crippled ankle, and the consequent appropriation of his room, but never would he forgive the merciless detail of that sketch.

"I'll carry easel and all into the parlor, and leave the door open so you can hear what they all say," said the Little Doctor, cheerfully. "I wish Cecil could be here to-day. I always miss Cecil when there's anything especial going on in the way of fun."

"Yes?" answered Chip, and made himself another cigarette. He would be glad when he could hobble out to some lonely spot and empty his soul of the profane language stored away opposite the name of Dr. Cecil Granthum. There is so little comfort in swearing all inside, when one feels deeply upon a subject.

"It's a wonder you wouldn't send for him if you miss him that bad," he remarked, after a minute, hoping the Little Doctor would not find anything amiss with his tone, which he meant should be cordial and interested—and which evinced plenty of interest, of a kind, but was curiously lacking in cordiality.

"I did beg, and tease, and entreat—but Cecil's in a hospital—as a physician, you understand, not as a patient, and can't get off just yet. In a month or two, perhaps——"

Dinner, called shrilly by the Countess, interrupted her, and she flitted out of the room looking as little like a lovelorn maiden as she did like a doctor—which was little indeed.

"She begged, and teased, and entreated," repeated Chip, savagely to himself when the door closed upon her, and fell into gloomy meditation, which left him feeling that there was no good thing in this wicked world—no, not one—that was not appropriated by some one with not sense enough to understand and appreciate his blessing.

After dinner the Little Doctor spoke to the unsuspecting critics.

"That picture which I started a couple of weeks ago is finished at last, and I want you good people to come and tell me what you think of it. I want you all—you, Slim, and Louise, you are to come and give your opinion."

"Well, I don't know the first thing about paintin'," remonstrated the Countess, coming in from the kitchen.

The Old Man lighted his pipe and followed her into the parlor with the others, and Slim rolled a cigarette to hide his embarrassment, for the rôle of art critic was new to him.

There was some nervousness in the Little Doctor's manner as she set the easel to her liking and drew aside the curtain. She did not mean to be theatrical about it, but Chip, watching through the open door, fancied so, and let his lip curl a trifle. He was not in a happy frame of mind just then.

A silence fell upon the group. The Old Man took his pipe from his mouth and stared.

The cheeks of the Little Doctor paled and grew pink again. She laughed a bit, as though she would much rather cry.

"Say something, somebody, quick!" she cried, when her nerves would bear no more.

"Well, I do think it's awfully good, Dell," began the Countess.

"By golly, I don't see how you done that without seein' it happen," exclaimed Slim, looking very dazed and mystified.

"That's a Diamond Bar cow," remarked J. G., abstractedly. "That outfit never does git half their calves. I remember the last time I rode through there last winter, that cow—doggone it, Dell, how the dickens did you get that cow an' calf in? You must a had a photograph t' work from."

"By golly, that's right," chimed in Slim. "That there's the cow I had sech a time chasin' out uh the bunch down on the bottom. I run her till I was plum sick, an' so was she, by golly. I'd know her among a thousand. Yuh got her complete—all but the beller, an', by golly, yuh come blame near gittin' that, too!" Slim, always slow and very much in earnest, gradually became infused with the spirit of the scene. "Jest look at that ole gray sinner with his nose r'ared straight up in the air over there! By golly, he's callin' all his wife's relations t' come an' help 'em out. He's thinkin' the ole Diamon' Bar's goin' t' be one too many fer 'em. She shore looks fighty, with 'er head down an' 'er eyes rollin' all ways t' oncet, ready fer the first darn cuss that makes a crooked move! An' they know it, too, by golly, er they wouldn't hang back like they're a-doin'. I'd shore like t' be cached behind that ole pine stub with a thirty-thirty an' a fist full uh shells—I'd shore make a scatteration among 'em! A feller could easy——"

"But, Slim, they're nothing but paint!" The Little Doctor's eyes were shining.

Slim turned red and grinned sheepishly at the others.

"I kinda fergot it wasn't nothin' but a pitcher," he stammered, apologetically.

"That is the gist of the whole matter," said Dunk.

"You couldn't ask for a greater compliment, or higher praise, than that, Miss Della. One forgets that it is a picture. One only feels a deep longing for a good rifle. You must let me take it with me to Butte. That picture will make you famous among cattlemen, at least. That is to say, out West, here. And if you will sell it I am positive I can get you a high price for it."

The eyes of the Little Doctor involuntarily sought the Morris chair in the next room; but Chip was looking out across the coulee, as he had a habit of doing lately, and seemed not to hear what was going on in the parlor. He was indifference personified, if one might judge from his outward appearance. The Little Doctor turned her glance resentfully to her brother's partner.

"Do you mean all that?" she demanded of him.

"I certainly do. It is great, Miss Della. I admit that it is not quite like your other work; the treatment seems different, in places, and—er—stronger. It is the best picture of the kind that I have ever seen, I think. It holds one, in a way——"

"By golly, I bet Chip took a pitcher uh that!" exclaimed Slim, who had been doing some hard thinking. "He was tellin' us last winter about ridin' up on that ole Diamon' Bar cow with a pack uh wolves around her, an' her a-standin' 'em off, an' he shot two uh the wolves. Yes, sir; Chip jest about got a snap shot of 'em."

"Well, doggone it! what if he did?" The Old Man turned jealously upon him. "It ain't everyone that kin paint like that, with nothin' but a little kodak picture t' go by. Doggone it! I don't care if Dell had a hull apurn full uh kodak pictures that Chip took—it's a rattlin' good piece uh work, all the same."

"I ain't sayin' anything agin' the pitcher," retorted Slim. "I was jest wonderin' how she happened t' git that cow down s' fine, brand 'n all, without some kind uh pattern t' go by. S' fur 's the pitcher goes, it's about as good 's kin be did with paint, I guess. I ain't ever seen anything in the pitcher line that looked any natcherler."

"Well, I do think it's just splendid!" gurgled the

Countess. "It's every bit as good 's the one Mary got with a year's subscription t' the *Household Treasure* fer fifty cents. That one's got some hounds chasin' a deer and a man hidin' in the bushes, sost yuh kin jest see his head. It's an awful purty pitcher, but this one's jest as good. I do b'lieve it's a little bit better, if anything. Mary's has got some awful nice, green grass, an' the sky's an awful purty blue—jest about the color uh my blue silk waist. But yuh can't expect t' have grass an' sky like that in the winter, an' this is more of a winter pitcher. It looks awful cold an' lonesome, somehow, an' it makes yuh want t' cry, if yuh look at it long enough."

The critics stampeded, as they always did when the Countess began to talk.

"You better let Dunk take it with him, Dell," was the parting advice of the Old Man.

CHAPTER XIV.

Convalescence.

"You don't mind, do you?" The Little Doctor was visibly uneasy.

"Mind what?" Chip's tone was one of elaborate unconsciousness. "Mind Dunk's selling the picture for you? Why should I? It's yours, you know."

"I think you have some interest in it yourself," she said, without looking at him. "You don't think I mean to—to——"

"I don't think anything, except that it's your picture, and I put in a little time meddling with your property for want of something else to do. All I painted doesn't cover one quarter of the canvas, and I guess you've done enough for me to more than make up. I guess you needn't worry over that cow and calf—you're welcome to them both; and if you can get a bounty on those five wolves, I'll be glad to have you. Just keep still about my part of it."

Chip really felt that way about it, after the first dash of wounded pride. He could never begin to square accounts with the Little Doctor, anyhow, and he was proud that he could do something for her, even if it was nothing more than fixing up a picture so that it rose considerably above mediocrity. He had meant it that way all along, but the suspicion that she was quite ready to appropriate his work rather shocked him, just at first. No one likes having a gift we joy in bestowing calmly taken from our hands before it has been offered. He wanted her to have the picture for her very own—but—but—— He had not thought of the possibility of her selling it, or of Dunk as her agent. It was all right, of course, if she wanted to do that with it, but—— There was something about it that hurt, and the hurt of it was not less, simply because he could not locate the pain.

His mind fidgeted with the subject. If he could have saddled Silver and gone for a long gallop over the prairie land, he could have grappled with his rebellious inner self and choked to death several unwelcome emotions, he thought. But there was Silver, crippled and swung uncomfortably in canvas wrappings in the box stall, and here was himself, crippled and held day after day in one room and one chair—albeit a very pleasant room and a very comfortable chair—and a gallop as impossible to one of them as to the other.

"I do wish——" The Little Doctor checked herself abruptly, and hummed a bit of coon song.

"What do you wish?" Chip pushed his thoughts behind him, and tried to speak in his usual manner.

"Nothing much. I was just wishing Cecil could see 'The Last Stand.' "

Chip said absolutely nothing for five minutes, and for an excellent reason. There was not a single thought during that time which would sound pretty if put into words, and he had no wish to shock the Little Doctor.

After that day a constraint fell upon them both, which each felt keenly and neither cared to explain away. "The Last Stand" was tacitly dismissed from their conversation, of which there grew less and less as the days passed.

Then came a time when Chip strongly resented being looked upon as an invalid, and Johnny was sent home, greatly to his sorrow.

Chip hobbled about the house on crutches, and chafed and fretted, and managed to be very miserable indeed because he could not get out and ride and clear his brain and heart of some of their hurt—for it had come to just that; he had been compelled to own that there was a hurt which would not heal in a hurry.

It was a very bitter young man who, lounging in the big chair by the window one day, suddenly snorted contempt at a Western story he had been reading and cast the magazine—one of the Six Leading—clean into the parlor where it sprawled its artistic leaves in the middle of the floor. The Little Doctor was somewhere—he never seemed to know just where, nowadays—and the house was lonesome as an isolated peak in the Bad Lands.

"I wish I had the making of the laws. I'd put a

bounty on all the darn fools that think they can write cowboy stories just because they rode past a round-up once, on a fast train," he growled, reaching for his tobacco sack. "Huh! I'd like to meet up with the yahoo that wrote that rank yarn! I'd ask him where he got his lack of information. Huh! A cow-puncher togged up like he was going after the snakiest bronk in the country, when he was only going to drive to town in a buckboard! 'His pistol belt and dirk and leathern chaps'—oh, Lord; oh, Lord! And spurs! I wonder if he thinks it takes spurs to ride a buckboard? Do they think, back East, that spurs grow on a man's heels out here and won't come off? Do they think we *sleep* in 'em, I wonder?" He drew a match along the arm of the chair where the varnish was worn off. "They think all a cow-puncher has to do is eat and sleep and ride fat horses. I'd like to tell some of them a few things that they don't——"

"I've brought you a caller, Chip. Aren't you glad to see him?" It was the Little Doctor at the window, and the laugh he loved was in her voice and in her eyes, that it hurt him to meet, lately.

The color surged to his face, and he leaned from the window, his thin, white hand outstretched caressingly.

"I'd tell a man!" he said, and choked a little over it. "Silver, old boy!"

Silver, nickering softly, limped forward and nestled his nose in the palm of his master.

"He's been out in the corral for several days, but I didn't tell you—I wanted it for a surprise," said the Little Doctor. "This is his longest trip, but he'll soon be well now."

"Yes; I'd give a good deal if I could walk as well as he can," said Chip, gloomily.

"He wasn't hurt as badly as you were. You ought to be thankful you can walk at all, and that you won't limp all your life. I was afraid for a while, just at first——"

"You were? Why didn't you tell me?" Chip's eyes were fixed sternly upon her.

"Because I didn't want to. It would only have

made matters worse, anyway. And you won't limp, you know, if you're careful for a while longer. I'm going to get Silver his sugar. He has sugar every day."

Silver lifted his head and looked after her inquiringly, whinnied complainingly, and prepared to follow as best he could.

"Silver—oh, Silver!" Chip snapped his fingers to attract his attention. "Hang the luck, come back here! Would you throw down your best friend for that girl? Has she got to have you, too?" His voice grew wistfully rebellious. "You're mine. Come back here, you little fool—she doesn't care."

Silver stopped at the corner, swung his head and looked back at Chip, beckoning, coaxing, swearing under his breath. His eyes sought for sign of his goddess, who had disappeared most mysteriously. Throwing up his head, he sent a protest shrilling through the air, and looked no more at Chip.

"I'm—coming, now be still. Oh, don't you dare paw with your lame leg! Why didn't you stay with your master?"

"He's no use for his master, any more," said Chip, with a hurt laugh. "A woman always does play the—mischief, somehow. I wonder why? They look innocent enough."

"Wait till your turn comes, and perhaps you'll learn why," retorted she.

Chip, knowing that his turn had come, and come to tarry, found nothing to say.

"Beside," continued the Little Doctor, "Silver didn't want me so much—it was the sugar. I hope you aren't jealous of me, because I know his heart is big enough to hold us both."

She stayed a long half hour, and was so gay that it seemed like old times to listen to her laugh and watch her dimples while she talked. Chip forgot that he had a quarrel with fate, and he also forgot Dr. Cecil Granthum, of Gilroy, Ohio—until Slim rode up and handed the Little Doctor a letter addressed in that bold, up-and-down writing that Chip considered a little the ugliest specimen of chirography he had ever seen in his life.

"It's from Cecil," said the Little Doctor, simply and unnecessarily, and led Silver back down the hill.

Chip, gazing at that tiresome bluff across the coulee, renewed his quarrel with fate.

CHAPTER XV.

The Spoils of Victory.

"I wish, while I'm gone, you'd paint me another picture. Will you, *please?*"

When a girl has big, gray eyes that half convince you they are not gray at all, but brown, or blue, at times, and a way of using them that makes a fellow heady, like champagne, and a couple of dimples that will dodge into her cheeks just when a fellow is least prepared to resist them—why, what can a fellow do but knuckle under and say yes, especially when she lets her head tip to one side a little and says "please" like that?

Chip tried not to look at her, but he couldn't help himself very well while she stood directly in front of him. He compromised weakly instead of refusing point-blank, as he told himself he wanted to do.

"I don't know—maybe I can't, again."

"Maybe you can, though. Here's an eighteen by

twenty-four canvas, and here are all the paints I have in the house, and the brushes. I'll expect to see something worth while, when I return."

"Well, but if I can't——"

"Look here. Straight in the eye, if you please! Now, will you *try?*"

Chip, looking into her eyes that were laughing, but with a certain earnestness behind the laugh, threw up his hands—mentally, you know.

"Yes, I'll try. How long are you going to be gone?"

"Oh, perhaps a week," she said, lightly, and Chip's heart went heavy.

"You may paint any kind of picture you like, but I'd rather you did something like 'The Last Stand'—only better. And put your brand, as you call it, in one corner."

"You won't sell it, will you?" The words slipped out before he knew.

"No—no, I won't sell it, for it won't be mine. It's for yourself this time."

"Then there won't be any picture," said Chip, shortly.

"Oh, yes, there will," smiled the Little Doctor, sweetly, and went away before he could contradict her.

Perhaps a week! Heavens, that was seven days, and every day had at least sixteen waking hours. How would it be when it was years, then? When Dr. Cecil Granthum—(er—no, I won't. The invective attached to that gentleman's name was something not to be repeated here.) At any rate, a week was a long, long time to put in without any gray eyes or any laugh, or any dimples, or, in short, without the Little Doctor. He could not see, for his part, why she wanted to go gadding off to the Falls with Len Adams and the schoolma'am, anyway. Couldn't they get along without her? They always had, before she came to the country; but, for that matter, so had he. The problem was, how was he going to get along without her for the rest of his life? What did they want to stay a week for? Couldn't they buy everything they wanted in a day or so? And the Giant Spring wasn't such great shakes, nor the Rainbow Falls, that they need to hang around town a week just to look at them. And the picture—what was he such a fool for? Couldn't he say no with a pair of gray eyes staring into his? It seemed not. He supposed he must think up something to daub on there—the poorer the better.

That first day Chip smoked something like two dozen cigarettes, gazed out across the coulee till his eyes ached, glared morosely at the canvas on the easel, which stared back at him till the dull blankness of it stamped itself upon his brain and he could see nothing else, look where he might. Whereupon he gathered up hat and crutches, and hobbled slowly down the hill to tell Silver his troubles.

The second day threatened to be like the first. Chip sat by the window and smoked; but, little by little, the smoke took form and substance until, when he turned his eyes to the easel, a picture looked back at him—even though to other eyes the canvas was yet blank and waiting.

There was no Johnny this time to run at his beckoning. He limped about on his crutches, collected all things needful, and sat down to work.

As he sketched and painted, with a characteristic rapidity that was impatient of the slightest interruption yet patient in its perfectness of detail, the picture born of the smoke grew steadily upon the canvas.

It seemed, at first, that "The Last Stand" was to be repeated. There were the same jagged pinnacles and scrubby pines, held in the fierce grip of the frozen chinook. The same? But there was a difference, not to be explained, perhaps, but certainly to be felt. The Little Doctor's hills were jagged, barren hills; her pines were very nice pines indeed. Chip's hills were jagged, they were barren—they were desolate; his pines were shuddering, lonely pines; for he had wandered alone among them and had caught the Message of the Wilderness. His sky was the cold, sinister sky of "The Last Stand"—but it was colder, more sinister, for it was night. A young moon hung low in the west, its face half hidden behind a rift of scurrying snow clouds. The tiny basin was shadowy and vague, the cut-bank a black wall touched here and there by a quivering shaft of light.

There was no threatening cow with lowered horns and watchful eye; there was no panic-stricken calf to whip up her flagging courage with its trust in her.

The wolves? Yes, there were the wolves—but there were more of them. They were not sitting in a waiting half circle—they were scattered, unwatchful. Two of them in the immediate foreground were wrangling over a half-gnawed bone. The rest of the pack were nosing a heap pitifully eloquent.

As before, so now they tricked the eye into a fancy that they lived. One could all but hear the snarls of the two standing boldly in the moonlight, the hair all bristly along the necks, the white fangs gleaming between tense-drawn lips. One felt tempted to brace oneself for the rush that was to come.

For two days Chip shut himself in his room and

worked through the long hours of daylight, jealous of the minutes darkness stole from him.

He clothed the feast in a merciful shade which hid the repugnance and left only the pathos—two long, sharp horns which gleamed in the moonlight but were no longer threatening.

He centered his energy upon the two wolves in the foreground, grimly determined that Slim should pray for a Gatling gun when he saw them.

The third day, when he was touching up the shoulders of one of the combatants, a puff of wind blew open the door which led to the parlor. He did not notice it and kept steadily at work, painting his "brand" into a corner. Beneath the stump and its splinter he lettered his name—a thing he had never done before.

"Well—I'll be—doggoned!"

Chip jumped half out of his chair, giving his lame ankle a jolt which made him grind his teeth.

"Darn it, Chip, did *you* do that?"

"It kind of looks that way, don't it?" Chip was plainly disconcerted, and his ankle hurt.

"H-m-m." The Old Man eyed it sharply a minute. "It's a wonder you wouldn't paint in a howl or two, while you're about it. I suppose that's a mate to—doggone you, Chip, why didn't yuh tell us you painted that other one?"

"I didn't," said Chip, getting red and uncomfortable, "except the cow and——"

"Yes, except the part that makes the picture worth the paint it's done with!" snorted the Old Man. "I must say I never thought that uh Dell!"

"Thought what?" flared Chip, hotly, forgetting everything but that the Little Doctor was being censured. "It was her picture, she started it and intended to finish it. I painted on it one day when she was gone, and she didn't know it. I told her not to tell anyone I had anything to do with it. It wasn't her fault."

"Huh!" grunted the Old Man, as if he had his own opinion on that matter. "Well, it's a rattling good picture—but this one's better. Poor ole Diamond Bar—she couldn't come through with it, after all. She put up a good fight, out there alone, but she had t' go under—her an' her calf." He stood quiet a minute, gazing and gazing. "Doggone them measly wolves! Why in thunder can't a feller pump lead into 'em like he wants t'?"

Chip's heart glowed within him. His technique was faulty, his colors daring, perhaps—but his triumph was for that the greater. If men could *feel* his pictures—and they did! That was the joy of it—they did!

"Darn them snarlin' brutes, anyway! I thought it was doggone queer if Dell could dab away all her life at nice, common things that you only think is purty, an' then blossom out, all of a sudden, with one like that other was—that yuh felt all up an' down yer back. The little cheat, she'd no business t' take the glory uh that'n like she done. I'll give her thunder when she gits back."

"You won't do anything of the kind," said Chip, quietly—too quietly not to be menacing. "I tell you that was my fault—I gave her all I did to the picture, and I told her not to say anything. Do you think I don't know what I owe to her? Do you think I don't know she saved Silver's life—and maybe mine? Forty pictures wouldn't square me with the Little Doctor—not if they were a heap better than they are, and she claimed every darned one. I'm doing this, and I'll thank you not to buy in where you're not wanted. This picture is for her, too—but I don't want the thing shouted from the housetops. When you go out, I wish you'd shut the door."

The Old Man, thoroughly subdued, took the hint. He went out, and he shut the door.

CHAPTER XVI.

Weary Advises.

"I have a short article here which may interest you, Miss Della," said Dunk, coming out on the porch a few days later with a Butte paper in his hand. The Little Doctor was swinging leisurely in the hammock.

"It's about the picture," he added, smiling.

"The picture? Oh, let me see!" The Little Doctor stopped the hammock with her toe and sat up. The wind had tumbled her hair about her face and drawn extra color to her cheeks, and she looked very sweet, Dunk thought. He held out the paper, pointing a well-kept finger at the place he wished her to read. There was a rather large headline, for news was scarce just then and every little thing was made the most of. The eyes of the Little Doctor clung greedily to the lines.

"It is reported that 'The Last Stand' has been sold. The painting, which has been on exhibition in the lobby of the Summit Hotel, has attracted much attention among art lovers, and many people have viewed it in the last week. Duncan Gray Whitaker, the well-known mine owner and cattleman, who brought the picture to Butte, is said to have received an offer which the artist will probably accept. Mr. Whitaker still declines to give the artist's name, but whoever he is, he certainly has a brilliant future before him, and Montana can justly feel proud of him. It has been rumored that the artist is a woman, but the best critics are slow to believe this, claiming that the work has been done with a power and boldness undoubtedly masculine. Those who have seen 'The Last Stand' will not easily forget it, and the price offered for it is said to be a large one. Mr. Whitaker will leave the city tomorrow to consult the unknown artist, and promises, upon his return, to reveal the name of the modest genius who can so infuse a bit of canvas with palpitating life."

"What do you think of that? Isn't the 'modest genius' rather proud of the hit she has made? I wish you could have seen the old stockmen stand around it and tell wolf stories to one another by the hour. The women came and cried over it—they were so sorry for the cow. Really, Miss Della, she's the most famous cow in Butte, just now. I had plenty of smaller offers, but I waited till Senator Blake came home; he's a crank on Western pictures, and he has a long pocketbook and won't haggle over prices. He took it, just as I expected, but he insists that the artist's name must be attached to it; and if you take his offer, he may bring the picture down himself—for he's quite anxious to meet you. I am to wire your decision at once."

The Little Doctor watched a pale green "measuring worm" loop its way hurriedly along the floor of the porch. She was breathing rather quickly and unevenly, and she seemed to be thinking very fast. When the worm, reaching the end, doubled out of sight, she started the hammock swinging and leaned back upon her cushions.

"You may tell him to come—I should like very much to see him," she said. "And I am very much obliged to you for the service you have performed."

She became very much interested in a magazine, and seemed to dismiss Dunk and the picture entirely from her mind. Dunk, after waiting till he was convinced she had no intention of saying more, went off to the stables to find a messenger for the telegram, telling himself on the way that Miss Della Whitmore was a very cool young person, and not as grateful as he would like her to be.

The Little Doctor went immediately to find Chip, but that young man, who had been just inside the window and had heard every word, was not so easily found. He was down in the bunk house, thinking things. And when she did find him, near supper time, he was so utterly unapproachable that her courage and her patience failed together, and she did not mention the picture at all.

"Hello, Doctor!" It was a heartening voice, sounding very sweet to the ears of the Little Doctor just then. She turned eagerly, her arms still clasping Silver's neck. She had come down to the corral to feed him sugar and tell him what a very difficult young man his master was, and how he held her at arm's length with his manner, and yet was nice and friendly and sunny enough—like the sun shining on an iceberg. But human sympathy was within reach of her hand, and it was much more satisfying than the mute sympathy of a horse.

"Weary Willy Davidson, you don't know how glad I am to see you! As the sayin' is: 'Yuh think of angels an' their opposets ain't fur off.' I *am* glad to see you."

"Dirt and all?" grinned Weary, for he had ridden far in the heat, and was dust-grimed and travelworn. He pulled the saddle off Glory, also, travelworn and sweat-grimed, and gave him an affectionate slap of dismissal.

"I'd chance money you wasn't thinking of me," he said, pointedly. "How is the old ranch, anyhow? Splinter up, yet?"

"You must think I'm a feeble excuse for a doctor," retorted she. "Of course he's up. He walks all around the house and yard with a cane; I promoted him from crutches yesterday."

"Good shot! That was sure a bad foot he had on him, and I didn't know—— What's he been putting in the time at? Making pictures—or love?"

"Pictures," said the Little Doctor, hastily, laying her cheek against Silver's mane. "I'd like to see him making love!"

"Yuh would?" said Weary, innocently, disregarding the irony of her tone. "Well, if yuh ever do, I tell yuh right now you'll see the real thing. If he makes love like he does other things, there won't any female girl dodge his loop, that's straight. What about the pictures?"

"Well, he drew a picture of J. G. sliding down the kitchen steps, before he was out of bed. And he made a picture of Dunk, that time Banjo bucked him off—you saw that happen, I suppose—and it was great! Dunk was standing on his head in front of his horse, but I can't show you it, because it blew out of the window and landed at Dunk's feet in the path, and he picked it up and tore it into little bits. And he doesn't play in Chip's yard any more."

"He never did," grinned Weary. "Dunk's a great hand to go around shooting off his mouth about things he's no business to buy into, and old Splinter let him down on his face once or twice. Chip can sure give a man a hard fall when he wants to, and not use many words, either. What little he does say generally counts."

The Little Doctor's memory squirmed assentingly. "It's the tone he uses," she said, reflectively. "The way he can say 'yes,' sometimes——"

"You've bumped into that, huh? Bert Rogers lit into him with a tent peg once, for saying yes at him. They sure was busy for a few minutes. I just sat in the shade of a wagon wheel and laughed till I near cracked a rib. When they got through they laughed, too, and they played ten games uh pool together that night, and got——" Weary caught himself up suddenly. "Pool ain't any gambling game," he hastened to explain. "It's just knocking balls into the pockets, innocent like, yuh see."

"Mr. Davidson, there's something I'd like to tell you about. Will you wait a few minutes more for your supper?"

"Sure," said Weary, wonderingly, and sat down upon the edge of the watering trough.

The Little Doctor, her arms still around Silver's neck, told him all about "The Last Stand," and "The Spoils of Victory," and Chip, and Dunk, and herself. And Weary listened silently, digging little trenches in the hard soil with the rowels of his spurs, and, knowing Chip as he did, understanding the matter much better than did the Little Doctor.

"And he doesn't seem to know that I never meant to claim the picture as my work, and I can't explain while he acts so—oh, you know how he can act. And Dunk wouldn't have sold the picture if he had known Chip painted it, and it was wrong, of course, but I did so want Chip to have some real encouragement so he would make that his life work. *You* know he is fitted for something better than cow-punching. And now the picture has made a hit and brought a good price, and he must own it. Dunk will be furious, of course, but that doesn't matter to me—it's Chip that I can't seem to manage."

Weary smiled queerly down at his spurs.

"It's a cinch you could manage him, easy enough, if you took the right way to do it," he said, quietly.

"Probably the right way would be too much trouble," said the Little Doctor, with her chin well up. "Once I get this picture deal settled satisfactorily, I'm quite willing to resign and let him manage himself. Senator Blake is coming to-morrow, and I'm so glad you will be here to help me."

"I'd sure like to see yuh through with the deal. Old Blake won't be hard to throw—I know him, and so does Chip. Didn't he tell yuh about it?"

"Tell me!" flashed the Little Doctor. "I told him Senator Blake was coming, and that he wanted to buy the picture, and he just made him a cigarette and said, 'Ye-e-es?' And after that there wasn't any conversation of any description!"

Weary threw back his head and laughed.

"That sure sounds just like him," he said, and at that minute Chip himself hobbled into the corral, and the Little Doctor hastened to leave it and retreat to the house.

CHAPTER XVII.

When a Maiden Wills.

It was Dunk who drove to meet the train, next day, and it was an extremely nervous young woman who met Senator Blake upon the porch. Chip sprawled in the hammock on the east porch, out of sight.

The senator was a little man whose coat did not fit, and whose hair was sandy and sparse, and who had keen, twinkling blue eyes which managed to see a great deal more than one would suspect from the rest of his face. He pumped the Little Doctor's hand up and down three times and called her "My dear young lady." After the first ten minutes, the Little Doctor's spirits rose considerably and her heart stopped thumping so she could hear it. She remembered what Weary had told her—that "Old Blake won't be hard to throw." She no longer feared the senator, but she refused to speculate upon what Chip might do. He seemed more approachable to-day, but that did not count—probably he was only reflecting Weary's sunshine, and would freeze solid the minute——

"And so you are the mysterious genius who has set the Butte critics by the ears!" chuckled the senator. "They say your cloud treatment is all wrong, and that your coloring is too bold—but directly they forget all that and wonder which wolf will make the first dash, and how many the cow will put out of business before she goes under herself. Don't be offended if I say that you look more capable of portraying woolly white lambs at play than ravening wolves measuring the strength of their quarry. I must confess I was looking for the—er—*man* behind that brush."

"I told the senator coming out that it was a lady he would have to make terms with. He would hardly believe it," smiled Dunk.

"He needn't believe it," said the Little Doctor, much more calmly than she felt. "I don't remember ever saying that I painted 'The Last Stand.'"

Dunk threw up his head and looked at her sharply. "Genius is certainly modest," he said, with a laugh that was not nice to hear.

"In this case, the genius is unusually modest," assented she, getting rather white. "Unfortunately for myself, senator, I did not paint the 'ravening wolves' which caught your fancy. It would be utterly beyond my brush."

A glimmering of the truth came to Dunk, and his eyes narrowed.

"Who did paint it for you? Your friend, Chip?"

The Little Doctor caught her breath at the venomous accent he employed, and the Old Man half rose from his chair. But Della could fight her own battles. She stood up and faced Dunk, tight-lipped and proud.

"Yes, Mr. Whitaker, my friend, Mr. Bennett, of whose friendship I am rather proud, painted the best part of 'The Last Stand.' "

"Senator Blake must forgive my being misled by your previous statement that the picture was yours," sneered Dunk.

"I made no previous statement, Mr. Whitaker." The Little Doctor's tone was sweetly freezing. "I said that the picture which I had begun was finished, and I invited you all to look at it. It was your misfortune that you took too much for granted."

"It's a mistake to take anything for granted where a woman is concerned. At the same time I shouldn't be blamed if I take it for granted Chip——"

"Suppose you say the rest to me, Dunk," suggested Chip from the doorway, where he leaned heavily upon his cane. "It begins to look as though I held a hand in this game."

Dunk wheeled furiously upon him.

"You're playing a high hand for a forty-dollar man," he grated, "and you've about reached your limit. The stakes are beyond your reach, my friend."

Chip went white with anger at the thrust, which struck deeper than Dunk knew. But he stood his ground.

"Ye-es? Wait till the cards are all turned." It turned him sick, though, the emptiness of the boast.

It was such a pitiful, ghastly bluff—for the cards were all against him, and he knew it. A man in Gilroy, Ohio, would take the trick which decided the game. Hearts were trumps, and Dr. Cecil Granthum had the ace.

The little senator got out of his chair and faced Chip tactfully.

"Kid Bennett, you rascal, aren't you going to shake hands?" His own was outstretched, waiting.

Chip crowded several hot words off his tongue, and gave up his hand for a temporary pump handle.

"How do you do, Blake? I didn't think you'd remember me."

"You didn't? How could I help it? I can feel the cold of the water yet, and your rope settling over my shoulders. You never gave me a chance to say 'God bless you' for that; you just coiled up your rope—swearing all the time you did it, because it was wet—and rode off, dripping like a muskrat. What did you do it for?"

"I was in a hurry to get back to camp," grinned

Chip, sinking into a chair. "And you weren't a senator then."

"It would have been all the same if I had been, I reckon," responded the senator, shaking Chip's hand again. "Well, well! So you are the genius—that sounds more likely. No offense, Miss Whitmore. Do you remember that picture you drew with charcoal on a piece of pine board? It stands on the mantel in my library, and I always point it out to my friends as the work of a young man with a future. And you painted 'The Last Stand!' Well, well! I think I'll have to send the price up another notch, just to get even with you for swearing at me when my lungs were so full of water I couldn't swear back!"

While he talked he was busy unwrapping the picture which he had brought with him, and he reminded the Little Doctor of a loquacious peddler opening his pack. He was much more genial and unpretentious since Chip entered the room, and she wondered why. She wanted to ask about that reference to the water, but he stood the painting against the wall, just then, and she forgot everything but that.

Chip's eyes clung to the scene greedily. After all, it was his—and he knew in his heart that it was good. After a minute he limped into his room and brought "The Spoils of Victory," and stood it beside "The Last Stand."

"A-h-h!" The senator breathed the word deep in his throat and fell silent. Even the Old Man leaned forward in his chair that he might see the better. The Little Doctor could not see anything, just then, but no one noticed anything wrong with her eyes, for they were all down in the Bad Lands, watching an old range cow defend her calf.

"Bennett, do the two go together?" asked the senator, at last.

"I don't know—I painted it for Miss Whitmore," said Chip, a dull glow in his cheeks.

The Little Doctor glanced at him quickly, rather startled, if the truth be known.

"Oh, that was just a joke, Mr. Bennett. I would much rather have you paint me another one—this one makes me want to cry—and a doctor must forego the luxury of tears. I have no claim upon either of them, Mr. Blake. It was like this. I started 'The Last Stand,' but I only had the background painted, and one day while I was gone Mr. Bennett finished it up—and it is his work that makes the picture worth anything. I let it pass as mine, for the time, but I never intended to wear the laurel crown, really. I only borrowed it for a little while. I hope you can make Mr. Bennett behave himself and put his brand on it, for if he doesn't it will go down to posterity unsigned. This other—'The Spoils of Victory'—he cannot attempt to disown, for I was away at Great Falls when he painted it, and he was here alone, so far as help of any kind is concerned. Now do make him be sensible!"

The senator looked at Chip, then at the Little Doctor, chuckled and sat down on the couch.

"Well, well! Kid Bennett hasn't changed, I see. He's just as ornery as he ever was. And you're the mysterious, modest genius! How did you come out after that dip into the old Missouri?" he asked, abruptly. "You didn't take cold, riding in those wet clothes, I hope?"

"I? No, I was all right. I stopped at that sheep camp and borrowed some dry clothes." Chip was very uncomfortable. He wished Blake wouldn't keep bringing up that affair, which was four years old and quite trivial, in his opinion. It was a good thing Dunk pulled out when he saw he'd got the worst of it, or there'd have been trouble, most likely. And Blake——

The senator went on, addressing the others.

"Do you know what this young fellow did, four years ago this last spring? I tried to cross the river near my place in a little boat, while the water was high. Bennett, here, came along and swore that a man with no more sense than I had ought to drown—which was very true, I admit. I had just got out a nice little distance for drowning properly, when a tree came bobbing along and upset my boat, and Kid Bennett, as we called him then, rode in as far as he could—which was a great deal further than was safe for him—and roped me, just as he would have roped a yearling. Ha! ha! I can see him yet, scowling at me and whirling the loop over his head ready to throw. A picture of *that,* now! When he had dragged me to the bank he used some rather strong language—a cowbow does hate to wet his rope—and rode off before I had a chance to thank him. This is the first time I've seen him since then."

Chip got very red.

"I was young and foolish, those days, and you weren't a senator," he repeated, apologetically.

"My being a senator wouldn't have mattered at all. They've been changing your name, over this side the river, I see. How did that happen?"

Again Chip was uncomfortable.

"We've got a cook that is out of sight when it comes to Saratoga chips, and I'm a fiend for them, you see. The boys got to calling me Saratoga Chip, and then they cut it down to Chip and stuck to it."

"I see. There was a fellow with you over there—Davidson. What has become of him?"

"Weary? He works here, too. He's down in the bunk house now, I guess."

"Well, well! Let's go and hunt him up—and we can settle about the pictures at the same time. You seem to be crippled. How did that happen? Some dare-devil performance, I expect."

The senator smiled reassuringly at the Little Doctor and got Chip out of the house and down in the bunk house with Weary, and whatever means he used to make Chip "behave himself," they certainly were a success. For when he left, the next day, he left behind him a check of generous size, and Chip was not so aloof as he had been with the Little Doctor, and planned with her at least a dozen pictures which he meant to paint some time.

There was one which he did paint at once, however—though no one saw it but Della. It was the picture of a slim young woman with gray eyes and an old felt hat on her head, standing with her fingers tangled in the mane of a chestnut horse.

If there was a heartache in the work, if the brush

touched the slim figure caressingly and lingered wistfully upon the face, no one knew but Chip, and Chip had learned long ago to keep his own counsel. There were some thoughts which he could not whisper into even Silver's ear.

CHAPTER XVIII.

Dr. Cecil Granthum.

The Little Doctor leaned from the window and called down the hill to her recovered patient—more properly, her nearly recovered patient; for Chip still walked with the aid of a cane, though by making use of only one stirrup he could ride very well. He limped up the hill to her, and sat down on the top step of the porch.

"What's the excitement now?" he asked, banteringly.

"I've got the best, the most *splendid* news—you couldn't guess what in a thousand years!"

"Then I won't try. It's too hot." Chip took off his hat and fanned himself with it.

"Well, can't you *look* a little bit excited? Try and look the way I feel! Anybody as cool as you are shouldn't suffer with the heat."

"I don't know—I get pretty hot, sometimes.

Well, what is the most splendid news? Can't you tell a fellow, after calling him up here in the hot sun?"

"Well, listen. The Gilroy hospital—you know, where Cecil is"—Chip knew—"has a case of blighted love and shattered hopes"—Chip's foolish, man-heart nearly turned a somersault. Was it possible?—"and it's the luckiest thing ever happened."

"Yes?" Chip wished to goodness she would get to the point. She could be direct enough in her statements when what she said was going to hurt a fellow. His heart was thumping so it hurt him.

"Yes. A doctor there was planning to get married and go away on his honeymoon, you know——"

Chip nodded, half suffocated with crowding, incredulous hopes.

"Well, and now he isn't. His ladylove was faithless and loves another, and his honeymoon is indefinitely postponed. Do you see now where the good news comes in?"

Chip shook his head once and looked away up the

grade. Funny, but something had gone wrong with his throat. He was half choked.

"Well, you *are* dull! Now that fellow isn't going to have any vacation, so Cecil can come out, right away! Next week! Think of it!"

Chip tried to think of it, but he couldn't think of anything, just then. He was only conscious of wishing Whizzer had made a finish of the job, up there on the Hog's Back that day. His heart no longer thumped—it was throbbing in a tired, listless fashion.

"Why can't you look a little bit pleased?" smiled the torturer from the window. "You sit there like a—an Indian before a cigar store. You've just about the same expression."

"I can't help it. I never was fierce to meet strangers, somehow."

"Judging from my own experience, I think you are uncommonly fierce at meeting strangers. I haven't forgotten how unmercifully you snubbed me when I came to the ranch, or how you risked my neck on the grade, up there, trying to make me scared enough to scream. I didn't, though! I wanted to, I'll admit, when you made the horses run down the steepest part—but I didn't, and so I could easily forgive you."

"Could you?" said Chip, in a colorless tone.

"If you had gained your object, I couldn't have," remarked she.

"I did, though."

"You did? Didn't you do it just to frighten me?"

Chip gave her a glance of weary tolerance. "You must think I've about as much sense as a jack rabbit; I was taking long chances to run that hill."

"Well, for pity's sake, what did you do it for?"

"It was the only thing to do. How do you think we'd have come out of the mix-up if we had met Banjo on the Hog's Back, where there isn't room to pass? Don't you think we'd have been pretty well smashed up, both of us, by the time we got to the bottom of that gully, there? A runaway horse is a nasty thing to meet, let me tell you—especially when it's as scared as Banjo was. They won't turn out;

they just go straight ahead, and let the other fellow get out of the way if he can."

"I—I thought you did it just for a joke," said the Little Doctor, weakly. "I told Cecil you did it to frighten me, and Cecil said——"

"I don't think you need to tell me what Cecil said," Chip remarked, with the quiet tone that made one very uncomfortable.

"It wasn't anything so dreadful, you know——"

"I don't want to know. When is he coming, did you say?"

"Next Wednesday—and this is Friday. I know you'll like Cecil."

Chip made him a cigarette, but he hadn't heart enough to light it. He held it absently in his fingers.

"Everybody likes Cecil."

"Yes?" Secretly, Chip had his doubts. He knew one that didn't—and wouldn't.

"We'll have all kinds of fun, and go everywhere and do everything. As soon as the round-up is over, I think I'll make J. G. give another dance, but I'll take care that the drug store is safely locked away.

And some day we'll take a lunch and go prowling around down in the Bad Lands—you'll have to go, so we won't get lost—and we'll have Len Adams and Rena and the schoolma'am over here often, and —oh, my brain just buzzes with plans. I'm so anxious for Cecil to see the Countess and—well, everybody around here. You, too."

"I'm sure a curiosity," said Chip, getting on his feet again. "I've always had the name of being something of a freak—I don't wonder you want to exhibit me to your—friends." He went down the hill to the bunk house, holding the unlighted cigarette still in his fingers.

When Slim opened the door to tell him supper was ready, he found Chip lying on his bed, his face buried in his arms.

If Chip never had understood before how a man can stand up straight on the gallows, throw back his shoulders and smile at his executioner, he learned the secret during that twenty-two mile drive to Dry Lake with the Little Doctor. He would have shirked the ordeal gladly, and laid awake o' nights planning subterfuges that would relieve him, but the Little Doctor seemed almost malignantly innocent and managed to checkmate every turn. She could not trust anyone else to manage the creams; she was afraid Slim might get drunk while they waited for the train, or forget his duties in a game. She hated J. G.'s way of fussing over trifles, and wouldn't have him along. Chip was not able to help much with the ranch work, and she knew he could manage the horses so much better than anyone else—and Cecil had been in a runaway once, and so was dreadfully nervous behind a strange team—which last declaration set Chip's lips a-curl.

The woman usually does have her own way in the end, and so Chip marched to the gallows with his chin well up, smiling at his executioner.

The train was late. The Little Doctor waited in the hotel parlor, and Chip waited in the hotel saloon, longing to turn a deluge of whisky down his throat to deaden that unbearable, heavy ache in his heart—but instead he played pool with Bert

Rogers, who happened to be in town that day, and took cigars after each game instead of whisky, varying the monotony occasionally by lemon soda, till he was fairly sick.

Then the station agent telephoned up that the train was coming, and Chip threw down his billiard cue, swallowed another glass of lemon soda and gagged over it, sent Bert Rogers to tell the Little Doctor the train was coming, and went after the team.

He let the creams lope in the harness all the way to the depot, excusing himself on the plea that the time was short; the fact was, Chip wanted the agony over as soon as possible; nothing so wears a man's patience as to have a disagreeable duty drag. At the depot he drove around to the back where freight was unloaded, with the explanation that the creams were afraid of the train—and the fact of that matter was, that Chip was afraid Dr. Cecil might greet the Little Doctor with a kiss—he'd be a fool if he didn't—and Chip did not want to witness the salute.

Sitting with his well foot on the brake, he pictured the scene on the other side of the building when the train pulled in and stopped. He could not hear much, on account of the noise the engine made pumping air, but he could guess about what was taking place. Now, the fellow was on the platform, probably, and he had a suit case in one hand and a light tan overcoat over the other arm, and now he was advancing toward the Little Doctor, who would have grown shy and remained by the waiting-room door. Now he had changed his suit case to the other hand, and was bending down over—oh, hell! He'd settle up with the Old Man and pull out, back across the river. Old Blake would give him work on his ranch over there, that was a cinch. And the Little Doctor could have her Cecil and be hanged to him. He would go to-morrow—er—no, he'd have to wait till Silver was able to make the trip, for he wouldn't leave him behind. No, he couldn't go just yet—he'd have to stay with the deal another month. He wouldn't stay a day longer than he had to, though—you could gamble on that.

There—the train was sliding out—say, what if the fellow hadn't come, though? Such a possibility had not before occurred to Chip—wouldn't the Little Doctor be fighty, though? Serve her right, the little flirt—er—no, he couldn't think anything against the Little Doctor, no matter what she did. No, he'd sure hate to see her disappointed—still, if the fellow *hadn't* come, Chip wouldn't be to blame for that, and Dr. Cecil——

"Can't you drive around to the platform now, to load in the trunk?"

"Sure," said Chip, with deceitful cheerfulness, and took his foot off the brake, while the Little Doctor went back to her Cecil.

The agent had the trunk on the baggage truck and trundled it along the platform, and Chip's eyes searched for his enemy. They were in the waiting room; he could hear that laugh of the Little Doctor's—Lord, how he hated to hear it—directed at some other fellow, that is. Yes, there was the suit case—it looked just as he had expected it would—and there was a glimpse of tan cloth just inside the door. Chip turned to help the agent push the suit case under the seat, where it was an exceeding tight fit getting it there, with the trunk taking up so much room.

When he straightened up the Little Doctor stood ready to get into the buggy, and behind her stood Dr. Cecil Granthum, smiling in a way that disclosed some very nice teeth.

"Cecil, this is Mr. Bennett—the 'Chip' that I have mentioned as being at the ranch. Chip, allow me to present Dr. Cecil Granthum."

Dr. Cecil advanced with hand out invitingly. "I've heard so much about Chip that I feel very well acquainted. I hope you won't expect me to call you Mr. Bennett, for I shan't, you know."

Too utterly at sea to make reply, Chip took the offered hand in his. Hate Dr. Cecil? How could he hate this big, breezy, blue-eyed young woman? She shook his hand heartily and smiled deep into his troubled eyes, and drew the poison from his wounds in that one glance.

The Little Doctor plumped into the seat and made room for Cecil, like the spoiled little girl that she was, compared with the other.

"I'm going to sit in the middle. Cecil, you're the biggest and you can easily hang on—and, beside, this young man is so fierce with strangers that he'd snub you something awful if we'd give him a chance. He's been scheming, ever since I told him you were coming, to get out of driving in to meet you. He tried to make me take Slim. Slim!"

Dr. Cecil smiled at Chip behind the Little Doctor's back, and Chip could have hugged her then and there, for he knew, somehow, that she understood and was his friend.

I should like very much to say that it seemed to Chip that the sun shone brighter, and that the grass was greener, and the sky several shades bluer, on that homeward drive—but I must record the facts, which are these:

Chip did not know whether the sun shone or the moon, and he didn't care—just so there was light to see the hair blowing about the Little Doctor's face, and to watch the dimple come and go in the cheek next him. And whether the grass was green and the sky blue, or whether the reverse was the case, he didn't know; and if you had asked him, he might have said tersely that he didn't care a darn about the grass—that is, if he gave you sufficient attention to reply at all.

CHAPTER XIX.

Love Finds Its Hour.

"Bay Denver's broke out uh the little pasture," announced the Old Man, putting his head in at the door of the blacksmith shop where Chip was hammering gayly upon a bent branding iron, for want of a better way to kill time and give vent to his surplus energy. "I wish you'd saddle up an' go after him, Chip, if yuh can. I just seen him takin' down the coulee trail like a scared coyote."

"Sure, I'll go. Darn that old villain, he'd jump a fence forty feet high if he took a notion that way." Chip threw down the hammer and reached for his coat.

"I guess the fence must be down som'ers. I'll go take a look. Say! Dell ain't come back from Denson's yit. Yuh want t' watch out Denver don't meet her—he'd scare the liver out uh her."

Chip was well aware that the Little Doctor had

not returned from Denson's, where she had been summoned to attend one of the children, who had run a rusty nail into her foot. She had gone alone, for Dr. Cecil was learning to make bread, and had refused to budge from the kitchen till her first batch was safely baked.

Chip limped hurriedly to the corral, and two minutes later was clattering down the coulee upon Blazes, after the runaway.

Denver was a beautiful bay stallion, the pride and terror of the ranch. He was noted for his speed and his vindictive hatred of the more plebeian horses, scarcely one of which but had, at some time, felt his teeth in their flesh—and he was hated and feared by them all.

He stopped at the place where the trail forked, tossed his crinkly mane triumphantly and looked back. Freedom was sweet to him—sweet as it was rare. His world was a roomy box stall with a small, high corral adjoining it for exercise, with an occasional day in the little pasture as a great treat. Two miles was a long, long way from home, it seemed to him. He watched the hill behind a moment, threw up his head and trotted off up the trail to Denson's.

Chip, galloping madly, caught a glimpse of the fugitive a mile away, set his teeth together, and swung Blazes sharply off the trail into a bypath which intersected the road further on. He hoped the Little Doctor was safe at Denson's, but at that very moment he saw her ride slowly over a distant ridge.

Now there was a race; Denver, cantering gleefully down the trail, Chip spurring desperately across the prairie.

The Little Doctor had disappeared into a hollow with Concho pacing slowly, half asleep, the reins drooping low on his neck. The Little Doctor loved to dream along the road, and Concho had learned to do likewise—and to enjoy it very much.

At the crest of the next hill she looked up, saw herself the apex of a rapidly shortening triangle, and grasped instantly the situation; she had peeped admiringly and fearsomely between the stout rails of the little, round corral too often not to know Denver when she saw him, and in a panic turned from the trail toward Chip. Concho was rudely awakened by a stinging blow from her whip—a blow which filled him with astonishment and reproach. He laid back his ears and galloped angrily—not in the path—the Little Doctor was too frightened for that—but straight as a hawk would fly. Denver, marking Concho for his prey and not to be easily cheated, turned and followed.

Chip swore inwardly and kept straight ahead, leaving the path himself to do so. He knew a deep washout lay now between himself and the Little Doctor, and his only hope was to get within speaking distance before she was overtaken.

Concho fled to the very brink of the washout and stopped so suddenly that his forefeet plowed a furrow in the grass, and the Little Doctor came near going clean over his head. She recovered her balance, and cast a frightened glance over her shoulder; Denver was rushing down upon them like an express train.

"Get off—your—*h-o-r-s-e!*" shouted Chip, mak-

"THROWING HERSELF FROM THE SADDLE, SHE SLID PRECIPITATELY INTO THE WASHOUT, JUST AS DENVER THUNDERED UP."

Page 253

ing a trumpet of his hands. "Fight Denver off—with—your whip!"

The last command the Little Doctor did not hear distinctly. The first she made haste to obey. Throwing herself from the saddle, she slid precipitately into the washout just as Denver thundered up, snorting a challenge. Concho, scared out of his wits, turned and tore off down the washout, whipped around the end of it and made for home, his enemy at his heels and Chip after the two of them, leaning low over his horse as Blazes, catching the excitement and urged by the spurs, ran like an antelope.

The Little Doctor, climbing the steep bank to level ground, gazed after the fleeing group with consternation. Here was she a long four miles from home—five, if she followed the windings of the trail—and it looked very much as if her two feet must take her there. The prospect was not an enlivening one, but she started off across the prairie very philosophically at first, very dejectedly later on, and very angrily at last. The sun was scorching, and it was dinner time, and she was hungry, and hot, and tired, and—"mad." She did not bless her rescuer; she heaped maledictions upon his head—mild ones at first, but growing perceptibly more forcible and less genteel as the way grew rougher, and her feet grew wearier, and her stomach emptier. Then, as if her troubles were all to come in a lump—as they have a way of doing—she stepped squarely into a bunch of "pincushion" cactus.

"I just *hate* Montana!" she burst out, vehemently, blinking back some tears. "I don't care if Cecil did just come day before yesterday—I shall pack up and go back home. She can stay if she wants to, but I won't live here another day. I hate Chip Bennett, too, and I'll tell him so if I ever get home. I don't see what J. G.'s thinking of, to live in such a God-forgotten hole, where there's nothing but miles upon miles of cactuses——" The downfall of Eastern up-bringing! To deliberately say "cactuses"—but the provocation was great, I admit. If any man doubts, let him tread thin-shod upon a healthy little "pincushion" and be convinced. I think he will confess that "cactuses" is an exceedingly conservative epithet, and all too mild for the occasion.

Half an hour later, Chip, leading Concho by the bridle rein, rode over the brow of a hill and came suddenly upon the Little Doctor, sitting disconsolately upon a rock. She had one shoe off, and was striving petulantly to extract a cactus thorn from the leather with a hat pin. Chip rode close and stopped, regarding her with satisfaction from the saddle. It was the first time he had succeeded in finding the Little Doctor alone since the arrival of Dr. Cecil Granthum—God bless her!

"Hello! What you trying to do?"

No answer. The Little Doctor refused even to lift her lashes, which were wet and clung together in little groups of two or three. Chip also observed that there were suggestive streaks upon her cheeks—and not a sign of a dimple anywhere. He lifted one leg over the horn of the saddle to ease his ankle, which still pained him a little after a ride, and watched her a moment.

"What's the matter, Doctor? Step on a cactus?"

"Oh, no," snapped the Doctor in a tone to take one's head off, "I didn't step on a cactus—I just walked all over acres and acres of them!"

There was a suspicious gurgle from somewhere. The Little Doctor looked up.

"Don't hesitate to laugh, Mr. Bennett, if you happen to feel that way!"

Mr. Bennett evidently felt that way. He rocked in the saddle, and shouted with laughter. The Little Doctor stood this for as much as a minute.

"Oh, no doubt it's very funny to set me afoot away off from everywhere——" Her voice quivered and broke from self-pity; her head bent lower over her shoe.

Chip made haste to stifle his mirth, in fear that she was going to cry. He couldn't have endured that. He reached for his tobacco and began to make a cigarette.

"*I* didn't set you afoot," he said. "That was a bad break you made yourself. Why didn't you do as I told you—hang to the bridle and fight Denver off with your whip? You had one."

"Yes—and let him gnaw me!"

Chip gurgled again, and drew the tobacco sack shut with his teeth. "He wouldn't 'gnaw' you—he wouldn't have come near you. He's whip trained. And I'd have been there myself in another minute."

"I didn't want you there! And I don't pretend to be a horse-trainer, Mr. Bennett! There's several things about your old ranch life that I don't know—and don't want to know! I'm going back to Ohio to-morrow, so there!"

"Yes?" He drew a match sharply along his stamped saddle-skirt and applied it to the cigarette, pinched out the blaze with extreme care, and tossed the match-end facetitiously against Concho's nose. He did not seem particularly alarmed at her threat—or, perhaps, he did not care. The Little Doctor prodded savagely at her shoe, too angry to see the thorn, and Chip drove another nail into his coffin with apparent relish, and watched her. After a little, he slid to the ground and limped over to her.

"Here, give me that shoe; you'll have it all picked

to pieces and not get the thorn, either. Where is it?"

"It?" sniffed the Little Doctor, surrendering the shoe with hypocritical reluctance. "It? There's a dozen, at the very least!"

Chip emptied his lungs of smoke, and turned the shoe in his hands.

"Oh, I guess not—there isn't room in this little bit of leather for a dozen. Two would be crowded."

"I detest flattery above all things!" But, being a woman, the brow of the Little Doctor cleared perceptibly.

"Yes? You're just like me in that respect. I love the truth."

Thinking of Dr. Cecil, the Little Doctor grew guiltily red. But she had never said Cecil was a man, she reflected, with what comfort she could. The boys, like Dunk, had simply made the mistake of taking too much for granted.

Chip opened the smallest blade of his knife deliberately, sat down upon a neighboring rock and finished his cigarette, still turning the shoe reflectively—and caressingly—in his hand.

"I'd smile to see the Countess try to put that shoe on," he remarked, holding the cigarette in some mysterious manner on his lip. "I'll bet she couldn't get one toe in it."

"I don't see that it matters, whether she could or not," snapped the Little Doctor. "For goodness sake, hurry!"

"You're pretty mad, aren't you?" inquired he, shoving his hat back off his forehead, and looking at her as though he enjoyed doing so.

"Do I look mad?" asked she, tartly.

"I'd tell a man you do!"

"Well—my appearance doesn't half express the state of my mind!"

"Your mind must be in an awful state."

"It is."

Two minutes passed silently.

"Dr. Cecil's bread is done—she gave me a slice as big as your hat, with butter and jelly on it. It was out of sight."

The Little Doctor groaned, and rallied.

"Butter and jelly on my hat, did you say?"

"Not on your hat—on the bread. I ate it coming back down the coulee—and I sure had my hands full, leading Concho, too."

The Little Doctor held back the question trembling on her hungry, parched lips as long as she could, but it would come.

"Was it good?"

"I'd tell a man!" said Chip, briefly and eloquently.

The Little Doctor sighed.

"Dr. Cecil Granthum's a mighty good fellow—I'm stuck on him, myself—and if I haven't got the symptoms sized up wrong, the Old Man's *going* to be."

"That's all the good it will do him. Cecil and I are going somewhere and practice medicine together—and we aren't either of us going to get married, ever!"

"Have you got the papers for that?" grinned Chip, utterly unmoved.

"I have my license," said the Little Doctor, coldly.

"You're ahead of me there, for I haven't—yet. I can soon get one, though."

"I wish to goodness you'd hurry up with that shoe! I'm half starved."

"Well, show me a dimple and you can have it. My, you are cranky!"

The Little Doctor showed him two, and Chip laid the shoe in her lap—after he had surprised himself, and the doctor, by planting a daring little kiss upon the toe.

"The idea!" exclaimed she, with a feeble show of indignation, and slipped her foot hurriedly into its orthodox covering. Feeling his inscrutable, hazel eyes upon her, she blushed uncomfortably and fumbled the laces.

"You better let me lace that shoe—you won't have it done in a thousand years, at that gait."

"If you're in a hurry," said she, without looking at him, "you can ride on ahead. It would please me better if you did."

"Yes? You've been pleased all summer—at my expense. I'm going to please myself, this time. It's my deal, Little Doctor. Do you want to know what's trumps?"

"No, I don't!" Still without looking at him, she tied her shoelaces with an impatient twitch that came near breaking them, and walked haughtily to where Concho stood dutifully waiting. With an impulsive movement, she threw her arms around his neck, and hid her hot face against his scanty mane.

A pair of arms clad in pink-and-white striped sleeves went suddenly about her. Her clasp on Concho loosened and she threw back her head, startled—to be still more startled at the touch of lips that were curved and thin and masterful. The arms whirled her about and held her against a heart which her trained senses knew at once was beating very irregularly.

"You—you ought to be ashamed!" she asserted feebly, at last.

"I'm not, though." The arms tightened their clasp a little.

"You—you don't *seem* to be," admitted the Little Doctor, meekly.

For answer he kissed her hungrily—not once, but many times.

"Aren't you going to let me go?" she demanded, afterward, but very faintly.

"No," said he, boldly. "I'm going to keep you—always." There was conviction in the tone.

She stood silent a minute, listening to his heart and her own, and digesting this bit of news.

"Are you—quite sure about—that?" she asked at length.

"I'd tell a man! Unless"—he held her off and looked at her—"you don't like me. But you do, don't you?" His eyes were searching her face.

The Little Doctor struggled to release herself from the arms which held her unyieldingly and tenderly. Failing this, she raised her eyes to the white silk handkerchief knotted around his throat; to the chin; to the lips, wistful with their well defined curve; to the eyes, where they lingered shyly a moment, and then looked away to the horizon.

"Don't you like me? Say!" He gave her a gentle shake.

"Ye—er—it doesn't seem to matter, whether I do or not," she retorted with growing spirit—witness the dimple dodging into her cheek.

"Yes, it does—it matters a whole heap. You've dealt me misery ever since I first set eyes on you—and I believe, on my soul, you liked to watch me squirm! But you do like me, don't you?"

"I—I'd tell a man!" said she, and immediately hid a very red face from sight of him.

Concho turned his head and gazed wonderingly upon the two. What amazed him was to see Chip kissing his mistress again and again, and to hear the idolatrous tone in which he was saying *"My* Little Doctor!"

THE END.